Anonymous

The Enchanter, or, Wonderful Story Teller

Iin which is contained a series of adventures, curious, surprising, and

uncommon: calculated to amuse, instruct, and improve younger minds

Anonymous

The Enchanter, or, Wonderful Story Teller
*Iin which is contained a series of adventures, curious, surprising, and uncommon:
calculated to amuse, instruct, and improve younger minds*

ISBN/EAN: 9783744750561

Printed in Europe, USA, Canada, Australia, Japan

Cover: Foto ©Andreas Hilbeck / pixelio.de

More available books at **www.hansebooks.com**

THE
ENCHANTER;

OR

WONDERFUL STORY TELLER:

IN WHICH IS CONTAINED

A SERIES OF ADVENTURES,

CURIOUS, SURPRISING, AND UNCOMMON;

CALCULATED TO

AMUSE, INSTRUCT, AND IMPROVE YOUNGER MINDS.

This Work to mend the Morals is defign'd;
To fhew to Youth the Paths of Wrong and Right;
To aid the Judgment and Improve the Mind,
And to convey Inftruction with Delight.

LONDON:

PRINTED FOR WILLIAM LANE,

AT THE

𝕸inerva-𝕻ref𝔰,

LEADENHALL-STREET.

M DCC XCV.

THE
ENCHANTER,
OR
WONDERFUL STORY-TELLER.

HISTORY of the PRINCESS HEBE,

AND THE

FAIRY ANGUILETTA.

HOW great foever fortune may raife thofe fhe favours, yet there is no happinefs exempt from trouble. Thofe who have any knowledge of the Faires, cannot be ignorant, that they, as wife as they feem, have not yet found out the fecret of fecuring themfelves from the misfortune of changing their fhapes fome days in each month, and affuming that of a beaft, bird, or fifh.

On thefe fatal days, when they are left a prey to the cruelty of men, it is often difficult for them to fave themfelves from the danger to which this hard neceffity expofes them.

One of them, who transformed herfelf into an eel, was unluckily taken by fome fifhermen, who put her prefently into a ciftern of water, in the middle of a fine meadow, where they kept the fifh referved for the king's table.

Anguiletta, which was the fairy's hame, found there a great many fine fifh, and heard the fifhermen fay one to another, 'That the king made that night 'a great entertainment, for which thofe fifh had been 'carefully picked out.'

What

What difmal news was this for the unhappy fairy, who accufed her fate a thoufand times, and fighed grievoufly when fhe got to the bottom, whither fhe went, that fhe might bewail her misfortune the more privately. The defire of avoiding the impending danger, made her look abroad on all fides, to fee if there was any way to efcape, and regain the river, which was but a fmall diftance from thence; but it proved all in vain, the ciftern was too deep to hope to get out of it without affiftance: and her fears increafed when fhe faw the fifhermen who took her, approaching, who put in their nets; and Anguiletta, by avoiding them, thought only to defer her death for fome time.

At that inftant the king's youngeft daughter, who was then walking in the meadow, came to the ciftern to amufe herfelf with looking at the fifh; the fun, which was then about fetting, fhining in the water, Anguiletta's fkin, which was ftreaked with gold, appeared fo bright, that the princefs took notice of it, and finding it very beautiful, bid the fifhermen take that eel, and give it her.

When the princefs had looked on Anguiletta fome time, moved with compaffion, fhe ran to the river-fide, and threw her in; which unhoped for fervice touched the fairy's heart with fo lively an acknowledgment, that fhe appeared that very moment on the top of the water, and faid to the princefs, ' I owe my life to you, ' generous Ploufina, (which was the name of the prin- cefs) ' which is a great happinefs for you. Be not ' afraid,' (continued fhe, feeing her going to run away) ' I am a fairy, and will fatisfy you in the truth of my ' words by what I will do for you.'

As they were ufed to fee fairies in thofe days, Ploufina took courage, and gave great attention to Anguiletta's agreeable promifes, and was about to make fome anfwer; when the fairy interrupting her, faid, ' Stay ' till you have received my favours, before you affure ' me of your acknowledgement. Go, young princefs, ' and come here again to-morrow morning: wifh for ' what you would have, and I will as foon accomplifh ' it; chufe either perfect beauty, a lively piercing wit,

or

' or vaft riches.' After thefe words, Anguiletta dived into the water, and left Ploufina very well fatisfied with her adventure.

She refolved to truft nobody with what had happened to her; for fhe faid to herfelf, ' If Anguiletta fhould ' deceive me, my fifters may think I have invented ' this ftory.'

After this fhort reflection fhe returned to her train, which confifted only of a few women, whom fhe found looking for her.

All that night the young Ploufina was engaged in the choice fhe was to make; that of beauty had a great fway with her; but as fhe had wit enough to defire more, fhe refolved to afk that favour of the fairy.

She rofe next day with the fun, ran to the meadow, as fhe faid, to gather flowers to make a garland, to prefent to her mother when fhe was up; but at the fame time, while her women difperfed themfelves in the meadow, which was all enamelled, to pick out the fineft and fweeteft flowers, the young princefs ftole to the river's fide, and found at the place where fhe had feen the fairy, a pillar of white marble, perfectly fine, which prefently opened, and the fairy came out of it; who was no longer a fifh, but a beautiful woman, of a majeftic air, whofe head-drefs and other apparel were covered over with jewels, ' I am Anguiletta, (faid fhe ' to the young princefs, who looked at her with great ' attention) and come to perform my promife; you ' have made choice of wit; you fhall have, from this ' moment, enough to deferve the envy of thofe who ' have hitherto pretended to it.'

The young Ploufina, after thefe words, found herfelf quite different from what fhe was an inftant before; fhe thanked the fairy with an eloquence, which till then fhe had never been miftrefs of; the fairy fmiling at the princefs's amazement to find fo much eafe in expreffing herfelf.

' I am fo well pleafed, (continued the kind Angui- ' letta) at the choice you have preferably made to beau- ' ty, which people of your age are fo much delighted

with

‘ with, that to recompenfe you, I will beftow that beau-
‘ ty upon you, which you this day have fo prudently
‘ neglected. Come again to-morrow at the fame hour,
‘ I give you that time to chufe how beautiful you would
‘ be.’

Then the fairy difappearing, left the young Ploufina
more pleafed than ever: the choice of wit was the effect
of reafon, but the promife of beauty flattered her heart;
and what reaches that, we are generally the moft affected with.

The young princefs leaving the river's fide, went to
receive the flowers her women prefented her with, of
which fhe made a very agreeable garland, and carried
it to the queen; but how furprifed was that princefs,
the king, and the whole court, when they heard the
young Ploufina fpeak with a grace that captivated their
hearts.

The princeffes, her fifters, ftrove in vain to think her
lefs witty than others; but were forced to yield, even
to their aftonifhment and admiration.

At night the princefs, poffeffed with the hopes of
being handfome, inftead of going to bed, fat up in her
clofet, which was hung with pictures, which reprefented,
under the figures of goddeffes, all the queens and princeffes of her houfe; and as all thofe pictures were very
fine, fhe hoped they might be affifting to her in the
choice of a beauty worthy of being afked of the fairy.

A Juno prefented herfelf firft to her eyes, fair, and
fet off with an air fit to reprefent the queen of the gods;
Pallas and Venus were by her: this piece being the
Judgment of Paris.

The young princefs was very much pleafed with the
pride and ftatelinefs of Pallas; but the beauty of Venus
inclined her there to fix her choice: neverthelefs fhe
paffed on to the next, where Pomona leaning on a bed
of turfs, under trees loaded with the fineft fruits, who
feemed fo charming, that the princefs, who fince the
morning knew every thing, was not furprifed that a
god had affumed fo many fhapes to ftrive to pleafe her.

Diana

Diana appeared next, as reprefented by the poets, a quiver on her back, and a bow in her hand, purfuing a ftag, and followed by her nymphs.

Flora appeared a little more careful; fhe feemed walking in a parterre, the flowers of which, though admirable, came not up to her complexion. Next her were the graces, who looked beautiful and engaging.

But the princefs was moft ftruct with a picture that hung over the chimney, which was the goddefs of youth; a charming air appeared through the whole figure; the hair was of the fineft white, the turn of her face admirable, the mouth delicate, the fhape and breafts perfectly fine and beautiful, and her eyes appeared more formidable to difturb our reafon, than the nectar fhe was feigned to pour out.

' I will (cried the young princefs, viewing the lovely ' portrait) be as beautiful as Hebe, and, if poffible, as ' lafting.'

After this, fhe went into her chamber, where the day fhe expected feemed too flow to fecond her impatience; but at length appeared, fhe returned to the river fide, where the fairy kept her word: and throwing fome water in Ploufina's face, rendered her as beautiful as fhe wifhed to be.

The firft effects of the fortunate Ploufina's charms, was the praifes of fome fea-gods that accompanied the fairy; fhe faw herfelf in the water, and knew not herfelf, her filence and amazement being then the only marks of acknowledgement. ' I have fulfilled all your ' defires, (faid the generous Fairy to her) you ought ' to be fatisfied, but I fhall not, till I have exceeded ' your defires by my bounty.'

' I give you wit and beauty, all the treafures in my ' difpofal, which are inexhauftible; wifh only for what ' riches you would have, and you fhall that minute ' obtain them, both for yourfelf, and whoever you ' think fit.'

The fairy afterwards difappeared, and the young Ploufina, who was then as handfome as Hebe, returned to the palace. All that met her were charmed. They told

told.

told the king of her arrival, who admired her himself, but knew her only by her voice and wit. She informed him that a fairy had bestowed those invaluable gifts on her; and that she would be called Hebe, because she perfectly resembled the picture of that goddess.

What new grounds of hatred were here for her sisters! Her wit gave them less jealousy than her beauty now.

All the princes who had been captivated by their charms, no longer balanced to become unfaithful; they forsook all the beauties of that court, no tears nor reproaches could stay those fickle lovers: and this proceeding, which at that time appeared so surprising, has since, they say, become common. In short, they all burnt for Hebe, whose heart remained insensible.

Notwithstanding the hatred of her sisters, she neglected nothing that might please them; she wished for so much treasure for the eldest, for to wish and give, was with her the same) that the greatest monarch of that country asked that princess in marriage, and the wedding was consummated, with great magnificence.

The king, Hebe's father, being inclined to raise a great army, the wishes of that fair princess crowned all his enterprises with success: his kingdom and treasury became thereby very much enriched, which rendered him a most formidable prince.

Nevertheless the divine Hebe, wearied with the hurry of the court, went to spend some months in a pretty box, some distance from the capital town, where she laid aside all magnificence, contenting herself with what was gallant, and of a charming plainness; nature there only embellished the walks, since art was not then used.

A wood surrounded this pretty retreat, the paths of which had something wild in them, divided by brooks and little rivulets, which formed natural cascades.

The young Hebe, walking often in this solitary wood, one day felt a secret grief and languishing, which never forsook her; she was ignorant of the cause of it, and sat herself down on the grass by the brook-side, the purling noise of which entertained her thoughts.

‘ What

' What chagrin, (faid fhe to herfelf) difturbs the
' excefs of my good fortune? What princefs in the
' world enjoys fo perfect a happinefs as myfelf? I have,
' by the fairy's bounty, all I wifh for; I can load all
' about me with riches; all that fee me, adore me; and
' yet my heart poffeffes not quiet thoughts. I cannot
' imagine whence proceeds the infupportable difquiet
' which hath, for fometime, oppofed the felicity of my
' life.'

Thus the young princefs continually reflected, till
at length fhe refolved to go to the river, to endeavour
to fee Anguiletta.

The fairy, accuftomed to flatter her defires, appeared
on the water, for it was one of thofe days when fhe was
metamorphofed into a fifh.

' I behold you always with pleafure, young princefs,
' (faid fhe to Hebe;) I know you are come from a very
folitary abode, and you appear to be languifhing, which
' is no way agreeable to your fortune. What ails you,
' Hebe? Tell me.'

' I ail nothing, (replied the young princefs, in con-
' fufion;) you have heaped too many favours on me,
' to want any thing to complete the happinefs which
' you have beftowed on me.'

' You fain would deceive me, (anfwered the fairy)
' I know very well you are not content; but what can
' you defire more? Merit my bounty by a fincere
' confeffion, and I promife to accomplifh your defires.'

' I know not what I would have, (faid the charming
' Hebe;) yet I am fenfible (continued fhe, louring her
' eyes) want fomething that is abfolutely neceffary to
' complete my happinefs.'

' Oh! (cried the fairy) 'tis love you defire; that
' paffion is only capable of making you think fo fan-
' taftically as you do.'

' A dangerous difpofition! (continued the young fairy.)
' You want love, you fhall have it; hearts are naturally
' but too much difpofed to it; but let me tell you, you
' will call on me in vain to put an end to that fatal

paffion

‘ paffion you think fo great a happinefs, my power not
‘ extending fo far.’

‘ That matters not, (replied the young princefs
‘ haftily, blufhing and fmiling at the fame time;) Alas!
‘ what fhould I do with all the riches you have given
‘ me, if I, in my turn, might not contribute to another’s
‘ felicity?’ At this difcourfe the fairy fighed, and
‘ fhrunk beneath the water.

Hebe returned to her folitude, with hopes that already
began to calm her troubles; the fairy’s menaces fomewhat difturbed her, but whofe wife reflections were foon
chafed away by others more dangerous, but much more
delightful.

When fhe came to the little box, fhe found a meffen-
ger from the king, who fent for her to come to court
the next day. The king and queen received her with
pleafure, and told her that a ftrange prince in his tra-
vels arrived at that court, they had a mind to make an
entertainment for him, to fhew other courts the magnificence of theirs.

The young Hebe, in a trouble fhe could not account
for, afked her fifter at firft if the ftranger was
handfome? ‘ You never faw any thing like him,’ (anfwered the princefs.) ‘ Defcribe him to me,’ (replied
the fair Hebe in diforder.)

‘ He is fuch as they feign heroes to be, (anfwered
‘ Ileria;) his fhape is fine, his air noble, his eyes full of
‘ fire, the power of which one of the moft infenfible
‘ ladies of the court has already confeffed: he has a
‘ very fine head of brown hair, and needs but fhew
‘ himfelf to gain the attention of all that fee him.’

‘ You fet him off to the beft advantage, replied Hebe)
‘ do you not flatter him?’ ‘ No, fifter, (anfwered the
‘ princefs Ileria, with a figh fhe could not reftrain:)
‘ Alas! you will find him but too worthy of pleafing.’

At night the prince paid the queen a vifit, who prefented him to Hebe, whom he had not feen; but never
were two hearts fo foon, or fo fenfibly touched, or ever
had more reafon.

The

The converfation was on different fubjects, but bright and agreeable, and fupported by all that vivacity the defire of pleafing could infpire.

When the queen retired, and the fair Hebe had time to make fome reflections, fhe was fenfible fhe had loft that tranquillity which fhe knew not the value of. 'O! Anguiletta, (cried fhe, as foon as alone;) what 'an object you permitted me to behold! Your fage 'counfels are deftroyed by his prefence. Why gave 'you not me ftrength to refift fuch charms? But per- 'haps their power exceeds that of a fairy.'

Hebe flept but little that night, fhe rofe very early, and the care of dreffing her againft the entertainment at night, amufed her all that day with an attention fhe was ignorant of till then; fhe being willing to pleafe for the firft time, the young ftranger, whofe defires were the fame, forgot nothing that might render him amiable int he charming Hebe's eyes. The princefs Ileria, on her part, neglected nothing that might pleafe; fhe was miftrefs of a thoufand beauties, and when Hebe was abfent, appeared the moft charming perfon in the whole world; but that princefs's prefence effaced them all.

At night there was a noble entertainment, followed by a fine ball, and the young ftranger had, without difpute, taken notice of the magnificence, could he have regarded any thing but the beautiful Hebe.

After the repaft there was a fine illumination, which gave as great light in the gardens of the palace, as if it had been day. They went to take a pleafant walk. The lovely ftranger gave the queen his hand; but that honour did not make amends for the chagrin of being feparated a moment from his princefs. The trees were covered with feftoons of flowers, and the lamps which gave the light were difpofed in fuch a manner as to reprefent bows and arrows, and other arms of love, and in fome places formed lines of writing.

They went into a little wood illuminated like the gardens, where the queen fat herfelf down by an agree-able fountain, about which there were placed feats of turfs, adorned with garlands of pinks and rofes. While

A 6 the

the queen talked with the king, with a great crowd of courtiers about them, the princesses amused themselves with looking at some characters the little lamps formed, the amiable stranger standing then by the charming Hebe, who casting her eyes cn a place where arrows were represented, read aloud these words, which were written under them:

" They are invincible."

' Such are the darts shot from the divine Hebe's ' eyes,' (said the unknown prince, looking on her tenderly.') The princess heard him, and was confused; but her embarrassment seemed to the prince a happy presage to his love, he having observed no anger.

When the diversions were over, the charms of the stranger had too sensibly touched the heart of Ileria, for her not to perceive he loved another. Before Hebe's coming to court, that prince had rendered her some little favours; but since that, had been altogether taken up with his tenderness for Hebe.

In the mean time, this young stranger endeavoured by his love to move the heart of the beautiful princess. He was in love, amiable, and his fate obliged him to love; and the fairy abandoning her to the inclination of her heart, what excuses were there for her to yield, who could not long hold out against herself?

The charming stranger told her he was a king's son, and was called Atimir, whose name was well know to the princes; for that prince had done wonders in a war between the two kingdoms; and as they had always been enemies, he went not by his true name at her father's court.

The young princess, after a conversation, wherein her heart had fully received the sweet and dangerous poison the fairy had spoken to her of, permitted Atimer to discover to the king his rank, and love; who transported with joy, ran to his majesty, and spoke to him with all the ardour his tenderness could inspire.

The

The king conducted him to the queen. Before this marriage, a lasting peace was made, and the beautiful Hebe was promised to her happy lover, as soon as he had received his father's consent. This news being spread abroad, the princess Ileria felt a grief equal to her jealousy: she cried and groaned, but was forced to constrain herself, and conceal her useless grief.

The charming Hebe and Atimir seeing one another every day, their tenderness augmented, and at that happy time, the princess could not comprehend why the fairies, when they would complete the happiness of mortals, should not use all their art and knowledge to make them love.

An ambassador from Atimir's father arrived at court, who had been expected with great impatience, and brought with him his consent; every thing was prepared for the marriage, and Atimir had nothing to fear; a dangerous state for a lover one would preserve faithful!

The prince thus assured of his happiness, became somewhat less sensible: one day, as he was looking for Hebe in the gardens of the palace, he heard the voices of some women in a summer-box of honey suckles; and hearing his name mentioned, which excited his curiosity to know more, he drew near to them, and heard the princess Ileria say to a person that was with her, ' I shall die
' before that fatal day, my dear Cleonice: the gods will
' not permit me to see the ungrateful man whom I love,
' united to the too happy Hebe: my torments are too
' grievous for my life to endure much longer.'　' But,
' madam, (answered the damsel) the prince Atimir is
' not unfaithful, he never made you any vows; fate
' alone is the cause of your misfortunes; and among so
' many princes that adore you, you may find more
' amiable than him, if a fatal prevention possesses not
' your heart.'

' Is there any in the whole world so lovely as him?
' (replied Ileria.) Powerful fairy! (added she, with a
' sigh, of all the favours you have bestowed on the for-
' tunate Hebe, I only envy Atimir's love.'

This

This difcourfe of the princefs's was interrupted by her tears Alas! how happy had fhe been, had fhe known how much fhe touched the heart of Atimir?

She ftarted up to go out of the box, and the prince hid himfelf behind fome trees. The tears and paffion of Ileria had foftened his heart, which he looked upon then only as compaffion, in favour of a beautiful princefs, whom he, againft his will, had made unhappy. Afterwards he went and found Hebe, whofe charms fufpended all other thoughts at that time.

In croffing the gardens to return to the palace, he found fomething under his feet, which he took up, and found it to be a fine pocket-book. It was not far off the box where he heard the converfation of Ileria, therefore he feared to fhew the pocket-book, left he fhould give Hebe any knowledge of that adventure; but hid it from that princefs, who was then employed in doing fomething to her head-drefs.

That night Ileria went not to the queen, who was told fhe was not very well after walking; and Atimir comprehended that fhe had a mind to conceal the diforder he had feen her in at the box, which thought redoubled his compaffion.

As foon as he got to his apartment, he opened the pocket-book he had found, and on the firft leaf found a cypher of a double *A*, crowned with myrrh, and fupported by too lovers, one of which feemed to wipe his eyes, and the other to break his arrows.

The fight of this cypher moved the young prince: he knew very well what Ileria meant; turned over the next leaf to know more, and found thefe words wrote on the back fide:

Almighty love, your charms difplay'd,
Which did my eafy heart invade:
Ah, cruel! thus your power to prove,
And blefs another with your love.

The hand, which he knew very well, informed him it was the princefs Ileria's book: he was touched with
thofe

thofe tender fentiments, which, far from being fupported by his love and care, were not fo much as fupported by hope. Thefe verfes put him in mind, that
before Hebe's arrival at the court, he thought Ileria
amiable; he began to look upon himfelf as falfe to that
princefs, and indeed, became too much fo to the charming Hebe.

However he oppofed the firft emotions; but his heart
was ufed to be fickle, and we feldom are capable of
breaking ourfelves of an ill habit.

He threw Ileria's pocket-book upon the table, refolved never to look into it; but took it up again in
fpite of himfelf a moment afterwards, and found in it
a thoufand things which completed Ileria's triumph over
the divine Hebe.

A thoufand confufed thoughts poffeffed the prince's
heart all night; in the morning he waited on the king,
who appointed the day of his marriage with Hebe.
Atimir anfwered with a confufion, which the king took
for a mark of his love. How hard is it to know the
hearts of men, fince that confufion was the effect of
his infidelity!

The king was going to the queen, and the prince was
obliged to follow him. He had not been there long,
when the princefs Ileria appearing with a languifhing
look, which the inconftant Atimir knowing too well the
caufe of, rendered her more lovely in his eyes; he
made up to her, talked to her a long while, and informed her he was not ignorant of her fentiments for him;
and afterwards explained himfelf to her with a tendernefs, which was an happinefs too great, and but
little expected by Ileria.

The charming Hebe came in at the fame time; the
fight of her made the princefs Ileria and the light Atimir
blufh. ' How handfome fhe is! (faid Ileria, looking
' on the prince with an emotion fhe could not conceal:)
' fly hence, Sir, or deprive me quite of life.' To which
the prince could make no anfwer.

When Hebe approached with an air and charms which
caft a thoufand reproaches on the ungrateful Atimir,

all

all which he could not support, he left the princefs, and told her he was going to difpatch a courier to the king his father; and fhe, for her part, being prepoffeffed in his favour, obferved not thofe looks he fometimes caft on Ileria.

While Ileria triumphed fecretly, the fair Hebe was told by the king and queen, fhe was to be married to Atimir in three days. But how unworthy was he then of the fentiments that news created in the heart of the lovely Hebe?

The prince, though poffeffed with a falfe paffion, fpent part of the day with Hebe; and Ileria, who knew of it, thought fhe fhould have died a thoufand times for jea-loufy; her love redoubling whenever fhe had any the leaft hope.

As the prince was going into his apartment at night, he received a letter from an unknown man, which he opened in hafte, and found thefe words in it.

' I Yield to a paffion a thoufand times more ftrong
' than my reafon; but fince it is in vain to conceal
' thefe fentiments from you, which chance hath dif-
' covered, come, prince, and know the refolution my
' tender love hath made me take. How happy fhould
' I be, if it coft me but my life!'

The perfon that brought this letter, told him, he was ordered to conduct him where the princefs Ileria waited for him. Atimir, without confidering a moment, fol-lowed him. After a great many turnings and wind-ings, they came to a fmall pavilion full of lights, which was at the end of a clofe-fhaded alley; where he found Ileria with only one of her women, the reft being gone to walk in the garden.

Ileria was fat on a crimfon cufhion, embroidered with gold; her drefs, which was both gallant and mag-nificent, was yellow and filver tiffue; her fine black hair was dreffed with ribbons of the fame colour as her clothes, intermixed with diamonds. At the fight of her, Atimir, afhamed of being falfe, fell on his knees by her, and Ileria looking on him with a tendernefs that fuffici-

ently betrayed the fentiments of her heart, faid,
' Prince, I fent for you, not to perfuade you to break off
' your marriage: I know too well 'tis refolved on: but
' fince fome words, which you were pleafed to flatter my
' misfortune and tendernefs with, do not permit me to
' believe you will leave Hebe for me; yet, (continued
' fhe, with tears that entirely feduced the heart of
' Atimir) I will facrifice to my love, without regret, a
' life you have rendered fo painful to me; and this
' poifon (fhewing a little golden box fhe held in her hand)
' fhall fecure me from the frightful punifhment of
' feeing you Hebe's fpoufe!'
    ' No, beautiful Ileria, (cried the fickle prince,) I
' will not be hers; I will leave her to pleafe you, whom
' I love a thoufand times better; and, notwithftanding
' my duty and faith fo folemnly given, I am ready to
' conduct you where nothing fhall conftrain our love.'
' Alas, prince! (faid Ileria, fighing,) fhall I truft my-
' felf with one fo falfe?' ' I will never be fo to you,
' (replied Atimir;) and the king, your father, who gave
' me Hebe, will not refufe me the lovely Ileria, when
' fhe fhall be in my power.' ' Let us go then, Atimir,
' (faid the princefs, after fome time of filence,) let us
' go where our fate hurries us; whatever I may fuffer,
' nothing can balance in my heart the fweet pleafure of
' being adored by the man I love.'
    After thefe words they confulted meafures for their
departure; and having no time to lofe, they refolved on
the night following.   They parted with a great deal of
reluctance; and, notwithftanding Atimir's oaths, Ileria
yet dreaded Hebe's charms, and was, the remainder of
the night, and the day following, continually poffeffed
with that fear.
    In the mean time the prince gave all neceffary orders
for their fecret departure; and the next night, when
every body was retired in the palace, went to Ileria's
pavilion in the garden, where fhe waited for him, attended
only by Cleonice.   They went away, and with incredible fpeed, got out of the kingdom.   In the morning,
this news was made known by a letter Ileria writ to the
                                                  queen,

queen, and one writ by Atimir to the king; which were
very moving, and easily discovered that love was the
dictator. The king and queen were in an extreme
rage; but words are not capable to express the piercing
griefs of the unfortunate and charming Hebe: how
great was her despair, and how many were her tears!
What vows did she not offer to the fairy Anguiletta, to
put an end to those cruel calamities she had foretold!
Hebe returned in vain to the river-side; Anguiletta,
who was as good as her word, never appeared, but abandoned her to the most frightful despair. The princess,
whom the ungrateful Atimir's good fortune had discard-
ed, took fresh hopes, and their cares and love seemed
new torment to the faithful Hebe.

The king desired her passionately to make choice of
a spouse, and oftentimes pressed her to it; but this duty
appeared too cruel to her tenderness; she resolved to
leave her father's kingdom, but before her departure,
went once again to find Anguiletta.

The fairy, who this time could not resist the tears of
the beautiful Hebe, appeared; at the sight of her the
princess renewed her tears, having no power to speak
to her. ' You now know, (said the fairy) what that
' fatal happiness is, which I was always willing to re-
' fuse you; but, Hebe, Atimir has punished you but
' too well for not following my advice; go, and avoid
' this place, which calls into your remembrance all your
' tenderness; you will find a vessel by the sea-side that
' will carry you to the only place in the world, where
' you may be cured of this unhappy passion that causes
' your despair; but remember, (added Anguiletta,
' raising her voice,) that when your heart is easy and
' quiet, you never seek after the fatal presence of
' Atimir, which will cost you your life.' Hebe wished
more than once to see that prince once again, whatever
that pleasure should cost her; but some remains of reason, and value of her honour, made her resolve to accept of the fairy's proposal. She thanked her for this
last kindness, and went the next day to the sea-side,
attended by those women she had the greatest confidence in.

There

There fhe found Anguiletta's veffel, all gilt with gold, the mafts of inlaid work, the fails of filver and rofe coloured tiffue, on which were wrote *Liberty*. The' failors jackets were of the fame colour as the fails, and every thing feemed to breath the fweets of Liberty.

The princefs went into a magnificent cabin, the furniture of which was admirable, and the paintings perfectly fine. She ftill afflicted herfelf as much in this new abode, as in her father's court; they endeavoured to divert her by a thoufand pleafures, but the ftate fhe was in, would not permit her to give any attention to them.

One day as fhe was amufing herfelf in looking on fome paintings in the cabin, in the place that reprefented a landfcape, fhe obferved a young fhepherdefs with a fmiling air cutting of nets, to fet fome birds at liberty that were taken; and fome of thofe little crea- tures that were efcaped, feemed to fly towards heaven with a wonderful fwiftnefs. The other paintings feemed to prefent fuch like fubjects; nothing feemed to fpeak of love, but all boafted of the charms of liberty; which made the princefs, in a melancholy tone, fay, ' Will ' my heart be always infenfible for fo fweet an hap- ' pinefs, for which my reafon makes fuch vain efforts.'

Thus the unhappy Hebe lived poffeffed with her ten- dernefs, and at the fame time with the defire of for- getting it

They had been about a month at fee when one morn- ing, as the princefs was upon deck, fhe difcerned at a diftance, a coaft that feemed very pleafant; the trees were of a furprifing height and beauty, and when they were nearer, fhe obferved they were full of birds, the plumage of which was of a bright fhining colour; they made a charming concert, their fongs being fo fweet, that they feemed as if they feared to make too great a noife.

When they arrived at this fhore, the princefs and her women landed; where fhe no fooner breathed the air of that ifland, but fhe felt a perfect tranquillity in her breaft, and fuffered herfelf to be furprifed by

an

an agreeable fleep, which clofed her eyes for fome
time.

This agreeable country, which to her was unknown,
was the Peaceable Ifland, which the Fairy Anguiletta,
who was a near relation to the prince and governor
there, had endowed for above two thoufand years, with
the happy gift of curing the. moſt unfortunate paffions,
and affuring them that gift ſhould ſtill continue; but
the difficulty was, to get to that ifland.

While the beautiful Hebe enjoyed a repofe ſhe had
not taſted the fweets of for fix months before, the prince
of the Peaceable Ifland, was taking the air in that wood
which bordered by the fea fide, in his chariot, drawn
by four white young elephants, and attended by his
court.

There he faw the princefs afleep: her beauty furprifed him. He alighted out of his chariot with a precipitation and vivacity he never felt till then. He took
at that fight all the love the charms of Hebe were worthy of infpiring. The noife awakened her, and ſhe
~~d~~~~~~~~~~r~~ eyes, difcovered a thoufand new beauties
to the young prince. He was about the fame age of
Hebe, which was nineteen; his beauty was perfect; a
thoufand graces were in all his actions; his fhape extraordinary, and his hair, which hung in large ringlets
down to the middle of his back, was of the fame colour
as Hebe's. His habit was made of feathers, of a thoufand different colours; he had it over a kind of cloak,
that trailed on the ground, made of fwans feathers,
buckled on the. fhoulders by very fine diamonds. His
belt was all of diamonds, on which hung, by chains of
gold, a fmall fabre, covered over with rubies. He had
a kind of head piece, made of feathers like the reſt, on
which was buttoned, by a very large diamond, fome
heron feathers, which fet it off with great fplendor.

This prince was the firſt object that prefented itfelf
to the young princefs when ſhe awakened. He appeared to her worthy of her regard; and it was the firſt
time in all her life that ever ſhe looked on any other
but Atimir with any attention.

‘ Every

'Every thing affures me, (faid the prince of the
'Peaccable Ifland to the princefs,) that you are the
'divine Hebe: alas! who befides could boaft fo many
'charms?' 'Who, Sir, could fo foon inform you,
'(anfwered the young princefs, getting up, and blufh-
'ing at the fame time,) that I was in this ifland?'
'A powerful fairy, (replied the young king) who,
'willing to make me the happieft of men, and this
'country moft fortunate, promifed me to conduct you
'here, and hath permitted me yet more glorious hopes.
'But I am very fenfible, (added he, fighing,) that my
'fate depends more upon your bounty than hers.'

After thefe words, to which fhe anfwered with a great
deal of wit, the prince defiied her to go into his chariot,
which fhould carry her to the palace, and out of refpect
went not into it himfelf: but as fhe underftood by his
difcourfe, and by his train, that he was the king of that
ifle, fhe obliged him to fit by her.

Never any thing appeared fo beautiful in one chariot;
all the prince's court at that fight could not forbear their
applaufes. While they were on the way, the young
prince entertained Hebe with a great deal of wit and
tendernefs, and the princefs, fatisfied to find her heart
at eafe, refumed all her vivacity.

They arrived at the palace, which was fome diftance
from the fea, and built all of Ivory, and covered with
agate, all the avenues to which were encompaffed with
fine canals.

The prince's guards were drawn out in all the courts;
in the firft they were cloathed in yellow feathers, with
head-pieces, bows and arrows, all of filver; in the fecond, they were cloathed in feathers of a fire-colour, with
gilt fabres, adorned with torquoifes. When they came
into the third court, the guards were cloathed in white
feathers, holding in their hands gilded and painted half
pikes, adorned with garlands of flowers; for in that
country they never were at war, therefore bore no terrible arms.

The prince alighted out of his chariot, and led the
amiable Hebe into a magnificent apartment. The
court

court was numerous, the ladies beautiful, the men gallant and handfome: and though all the inhabitents of the country were cloathed with feathers, the art of forming them in fhades made them very agreeable.

That night the prince of the Peaceable Ifland made a great entertainment for the beautiful Hebe, which was followed by a concert of fweet flutes, lutes, theorboes and harpfichords; for in that country they loved not noify inftruments. The fymphony was very fine; and when it had lafted fometime, a delicate fine voice fung fome words which declared the prince's paffion, while he gazed on Hebe, to perfuade her thofe words expreffed his thoughts.

As it was late when the mufic left off, the prince led the princefs into the apartment appointed for her, which was the fineft in the palace; there fhe found a great number of ladies, whom the prince had named to have the honour to be her attendants.

The prince left the beautiful Hebe, and was the moft in love of all men. They put her to bed; the ladies retired, and only left in the chamber thofe fhe brought along with her. ' Who could believe it, (faid fhe to
' them, when fhe was at liberty,) my heart is at peace!
' What God hath calmed my troubles? I love Atimir
' no longer; I can think, without dying with grief,
' that he is, perhaps, Ileria's fpoufe. Is not all I fee a
' dream? No, (faid fhe, recovering herfelf a little,)
' my dreams ufed not to be fo quiet.' In fhort, fhe returned Anguiletta a thoufand thanks, and then went to fleep.

The next morning when fhe awakened, as fhe opened the bed-curtains, the fairy appeared to her with a fmiling air, which fhe had never obferved in her face fince that fatal day fhe afked for love.

' At laft I have happily brought you hither (faid the
' amiable fairy to her) your heart is free, therefore
' will be content. I have cured you of a cruel paffion;
' but, Hebe, can I be affured that thefe terrible tor-
' ments, to which you have been expofed, will make

3   you

' you always avoid the fight of the ungrateful Atimir?'

The young princefs promifed the fairy every thing, and fwore both againft love and her falfe lovers. ' Re- ' member your promifes (replied Anguiletta, with an ' air that left an impreffion of refpect) you will perifh ' with Atimir, if ever you feek to fee him again. But ' every thing here ought to remove a defire fo fatal to ' your life.'

' I will no longer conceal from you what I have re- ' folved in your favour: the prince of this ifland is ' my relation; I protect his perfon and empire: he is ' young and amiable, and no prince in the world is ' more worthy of being your hufband. Reign then, ' beautiful Hebe, in his heart and kingdom: the king, ' your father, gives his confent; I was yefterday at his ' palace, and acquainted him, and the queen, your ' mother, with the prefent ftate of your fortune, which ' they have put abfolutely under my care.'

The princefs had a great mind to have afked the fairy about Ileria and Atimir; but durft not, after fo many favours, run the hazard of difpleafing her; therefore fhe only made ufe of all the wit fhe had be- ftowed on her to thank her.

Then fomebody coming into the room, the fairy dif- appeared. As foon as Hebe was up, twelve children, clothed like cupids, brought from the prince twelve bafkets of cryftal, full of the moft agreeable flowers, which only garnifhed fome jewels of a wonderful beau- ty. In the firft bafket that was prefented to her, this billet was found:

To the Divine HEBE.

' YESTERDAY I fwore a thoufand times how I ' loved; the fweet remembrance of which oaths ' will ever remain, fince they were dictated by love, ' and are fupported by your charms.'

After what the fairy had ordered the princefs, fhe comprehended that fhe ought to accept of her new lover, as of a prince that was shortly to be her husband.

She received the little loves very favourably; and had hardly dismissed them, when four-and twenty dwarfs, fantastically, but magnificently clothed, appeared loaded with new presents, that consisted of habits all of feathers: the colours and work of which, with jewels, were so fine, that the princess owned she had never seen any thing so gallant.

She made choice of a rose colour to wear that day; her head-dress was adorned with a plume of feathers of the same colour, and she appeared so charming with this new ornament, that the prince of the Peaceable Island, who came to see her when she was dressed, felt his passion redouble. All the court crowded to admire the princess. At night the prince proposed to the beautiful Hebe to walk in the gardens, which were admirable, where the prince told Hebe, that the fairy had fed him for four years with the hopes of her arrival in the Peaceable Island: ‘ but some time after (added the ‘ prince) when I pressed her on her promises, she ap- ‘ peared sad, told me, the princess is designed by the ‘ king, her father, for another, and not for thee: but if ‘ my knowledge deceives me not, she will not be that ‘ prince's, I will tell you more another time.’

‘ Some months after, the fairy came again : Fortune ‘ favours you, (said she to me) the prince that was to ‘ have been, will not be Hebe's spouse; and in a little ‘ time you will see here the most beautiful princess ‘ in the world.’

‘ Indeed, (replied Hebe, blushing,) I was to have ‘ been married to the son of a neighbouring king; but ‘ after a great many events, the love he bore my sister ‘ made him resolve to go away with her.’

The prince of the Peaceable Island said a thousand tender things to the beautiful Hebe on his happy fate, which according with what the fairy had told him, had brought her into this isle; and hearkened to him with so much the more pleasure, because this discourse inter- rupted the recital of her adventures; she feared she
should

should not be able to speak of her faithlefs lover, without difcovering the tendernefs fhe had had for him.

The prince conducted Hebe into a grotto curioufly adorned and embellifhed with the fpoutings of water.

The bottom of the grotto was dark; there were a great number of niches with ftatutes, reprefenting nymphs and fhepherds, which ware hard to be diftinguifhed.

When the princefs had been there fome time, fhe heard a delightful found of inftruments. A noble illumination that appeared all on a fudden, difcovered to her, that part of thofe ftatutes formed that concert; when the others came out, and danced fine and gallant dances, intermixed with tender and agreeable fongs; all the performers in this diverfion being placed at the bottom of the grotto, furprifed the princefs more agreeably.

After the dance, favages came in, and ferved up a ftately collation under an arbour of jeffamins and orange-flowers.

The entertainment was juft over, when all on a fudden the Fairy Anguiletta appeared in the air, in a chariot drawn by four fwans; and, defcending, pronounced to the prince of the Peaceable Ifland a charming happinefs, in telling him fhe would have him marry Hebe, and withal, that the princefs had promifed her to confent.

The prince, tranfported with joy, doubted at firft to whom he fhould return his firft thanks, whether to Hebe or Anguiletta; and though joy permits not of touching expreffions like grief, he acquitted himfelf, however, with a great deal of wit, and a good grace.

The fairy had no mind to leave the prince and princefs till the day appointed for their marriage, which was to be in three days; when fhe made them both coftly prefents, and went with them, who were followed by all the court, and a great many of the inhabitants of the ifle, to the temple of Hymen, which was made of olive branches and palms interlaced together, which, by the fairy's power, never faded.

B

Hymen

Hymen was there reprefented by a ftatute of white marble, crowned with rofes, and raifed on an altar adorned only with flowers, and fupported by a Cupid of an extraordinary beauty, who, with a fmiling air, prefented him with a crown of myrtle.

Anguiletta, who built this temple, was willing every thing fhould be plain, to fhew that love alone can render marriage happy. The difficulty is not to unite them together, but as the miracle worthy of a fairy, to join them together for ever in the Peaceable Ifland; which, contrary to the cuftoms of other countries, can make man and wife loving and conftant.

In this temple of Hymen the beautiful Hebe, led by Anguiletta, plighted her faith to the prince of the Peaceable Ifland, and received his with pleafure. She had not that involuntary inclination for him that fhe felt for Atimir; but her heart, then exempt from paffion, accepted of that fpoufe by the fairy's order, as a prince worthy of her by his perfon, and much more by his love. This marriage was celebrated by a thoufand gallant entertainments, and Hebe lived happy with a prince that adored her.

In the mean time, the king, Hebe's father, received ambaffadors from Atimir, who afked leave to marry the princefs Ileria (for his father was dead, and he left abfolute mafter of his kingdom) which was granted with joy.

After this marriage, the queen Ileria afked, by new ambaffadors, leave of the king her father, and queen her mother, to come to their court, to beg pardon for a fault which love had made her commit, and for which Atimir's merit was a fufficient excufe.

The king confented, and Atimir and his queen were welcomed on their arrival, with all the demonftrations of joy poffible.

A little after, the beautiful Hebe and her charming fpoufe fent their ambaffadors to the king and queen, with the news of their nuptials, which Anguiletta had informed them of before; yet, notwithftanding, they were not received with lefs pleafure and magnificence.

Atimir

· Atimir was then with the king when they prefented themfelves the firft time before him; the lovely image of Hebe was not to be abfolutely blotted out of an heart over which fhe had fo great a fway. Atimir could not forbear fighing when he heard of the happinefs of the prince of the Peaceable Ifland; he accufed Hebe a thoufand times of being inconftant, without thinking at the fame time of the caufe he had given her.

When the ambaffadors of the prince of the Peaceable Ifland returned crowned with honours, and loaded with prefents, they told their princefs the great joy the king and queen expreffed at their happy marriage.

But withal, (Oh! too fincere relation!) they acquainted Hebe, that the princefs Ileria and Atimir were at court. Thefe names, which were fo dangerous to their repofe, rendered her again uneafy; fhe was then unhappy, but mortals cannot long preferve a certain felicity.

She was not able to refift her impatience to return to her father's court; which was, as fhe faid, to fee the queen her mother: nay, fhe had even perfuaded herfelf into a belief of it; for how often do they who love deceive themfelves in their own thoughts?

Notwithftanding the fairy's threats to oblige her to avoid the fight of Atimir, fhe propofed that journey to the prince of the Peaceable Ifland, who at firft refufed her, for Anguiletta had bid him not let her ftir out of his kindom; but fhe continued her entreaties, and as he adored her, and knew nothing of her paffion for Atimir, he could not deny any thing to one he loved fo dear.

He thinking to pleafe the beautiful Hebe by a blind complaifance, gave orders for their departure; and never was feen more magnificence than in their equipage, and in their fhips.

· The wife Anguiletta, provoked at the little regard fhewn by Hebe and the prince to her orders, abandoned them to their fate, and never appeared to give them advice, which they had made fo little ufe of.

B 2

For the prince and princess, they, after a pleasant voyage, arrived at the court of Hebe's father; where the king and queen's joy to see that fine princess again was very great. They were charmed with the prince of the Peaceable Island, and celebrated their arrival by great rejoicings throughout the whole kingdom; only Ileria groaned when she heard of Hebe's return. And it was decreed, that when they should see one another again, no mention should be made of what was past.

Atimir asked to see Hebe, and seemed to Ileria to desire it with too great an ardour.

The princess Hebe blushed when he came into her chamber; they were both in a confusion, that all their wit was not sufficient to extricate them out of. The king, who was then present, observed it, and joining in their conversation, to make this visit the shorter, proposed walking in the gardens of the palace, and as Atimir durst not offer his hand to Hebe, he made her only a respectful bow, and so retired.

But what were the sentiments and ideas of his heart? All that lively and tender passion he had for Hebe, rekindled in his bosom; he hated Ileria and himself, and never was infidelity attended with more repentance and grief.

At night he waited on the queen, to whom Hebe was paying a visit: and not satisfied with looking at her, endeavoured to speak to her, which she always avoided; but still his eyes informed her too much for her quiet: he continued to shew, by all his actions, that hers had again resumed their empire over him.

Hebe's heart was alarmed; Atimir always appeared to her too lovely; she resolved to fly him, with as much care as he endeavoured to find out her. She never spoke to him, but before the queen, and then never but when she could not absolutely dispense with it; and was determined to persuade the prince, her husband, to return soon to their own dominions: but how difficult a thing it is to leave what we love!

One evening as she was engaged in these thoughts, and had shut herself up in her closet, that she might
think

think more at her liberty, fhe found in her pocket a
billet, that had been put into it unknown to her, which
fhe opened, and knew to be Atimir's hand, which gave
her inexpreffible trouble; fhe thought not to read it,
but her heart over-ruled her reafon, fhe looked it over,
and found thefe words in it.

FAIREST HEBE,

‘ YOU are too infenfible of my violent paffion, and
‘   ufe me with too much indifference: but fince
‘ your heart has, in its turn been falfe, and has fol-
‘ lowed but too clofe the example of mine, let it imitate
‘ it in its return. Forgive me my princefs, and per-
‘ mit me to refume thofe chains I once wore, when
‘ we partook of each other's pains and pleafures.’

‘ Oh, cruel! (cried the princefs) what have I done,
‘ that you fhould endeavour to rekindle in my foul a
‘ tendernefs that has caufed me fo much forrow?’ And
then her tears interrupted her difcourfe.

In the mean time Ileria languifhed under a jealoufy
too juftly grounded, and Atimir, hurried on by his love,
was unable to reftrain himfelf any longer. The prince
of the Peaceable Ifland began to difcover his paffion
for Hebe; but was willing to examine farther into
Atimir's conduct, before he fpoke of it to the princefs.
whom he adored conftantly, and whom he was afraid of
informing of that prince's love.

Some days after the receipt of this letter, there were
appointed courfes, when all the princes, and fprightly
youths of the court were to break lances in honour of
the ladies.

The king and queen honoured this diverfion with
their prefence. The beautiful Hebe and the princefs
Ileria were to beftow the prizes; which were a fword, the
handle and fcabbard of which were covered with diamonds; and a bracelet of moft curious diamonds.

All the knights named for the courfes appeared with
an extraordinary magnificence, mounted on very fine

horfes, bearing the colours their miftreffes delighted in, with devices on their fhields agreeable to the fenti- ments of their hearts.

The prince of the Peaceable Ifland was in a coftly drefs, mounted on a moft beautiful dappled horfe, with a fine long black tail and main: in all his equipage the rofe-colour appeared, which Hebe very much loved; and on his head-piece, which was very light, their waved a plume of feathers of the fame colour. He gained the applaufe of all the fpectators, and appeared fo handfome in his bright armour, that Hebe fecretly reproached herfelf a thoufand times for the fentiments fhe had the misfortune to have for another. His train was numer- ous, clothed after the manner of their own country, very gallant and ftately. An efquire carried his fhield, on which was this device, an heart pierced with an arrow, and a cupid fhooting a great number, to en- deavour to make frefh wounds; but all, except the firft, feemed to have been drawn in vain; thefe words were under-written:

I fear no other.

The colours and device of the prince of the Peaceable Ifland foon difcovered that he was Hebe's knight, and that as fuch he would enter the lifts. Every body was taken up with his magnificence, when Atimir came forward, mounted on a black fiery fteed, that ap- peared very ftately. His colour that day was dark green, intermixed neither with gold, filver, nor jewels, only he had a plume of rofe-coloured feathers on his head piece; and the other affected a great careleffnefs in his apparel; he had fo graceful a mien, and ma- naged his horfe fo well, and withal had fo lofty an air, that nobody could forbear looking at him: on his fhield, which he carried himfelf, appeared a love, who trampled his chains under his feet, and bound himfelf with others more weighty, with thefe words:

Worthy only of me.

Atimir's

Atimir's train confifted of the principle lords of his court, who were cloathed in dark green, laced with filver, and covered over with jewels; and though they were all handfome and well-fhaped, yet it was eafy to judge by that prince's air, he was born to command them.

The different emotions the fight of this prince produced in the hearts of Hebe and Ileria, and the jealoufy the prince of the Peaceable Ifland conceived, when he faw the plume on Atimir's cafque of the fame colour with his own, are not to be expreffed; the reading of the device compleated his rage, the effects of which he then ftifled till a better opportunity.

The king and queen foon took notice, both of the boldnefs and imprudence of Atimir, and were very angry; but it was not then a time to fhew it. The courfes began with the foundings of trumpets, and rended the air with their echoes; which were fine, and all the knights fhewed their addrefs; and the prince of the Peaceable Ifland, though poffeffed with an outrageous jealoufy, fignalized himfelf, and was proclaimed conqueror.

Atimir, who knew that the firft prize was to be given by Ileria, never difputed the victory with the prince of the Peaceable Ifland: he was declared victor by the judges of the field, and advanced gracefully, with the acclamations and praifes of all the fpectators, to the place where the king and princeffes fat, to receive the bracelet; which the princefs Ileria prefented to him, and he took with a good grace; then paying his refpects to the king, queen, and princefs, he returned to the lifts.

The melancholy Ileria obferving but too well the difdain the light Atimir fhewed for the prize fhe was to give, fighed grievoufly; and the beautiful Hebe felt in her breaft a fecret joy, which all her reafon could not refift.

The fecond courfe began with the fame fuccefs as the firft, wherein the prince of the Peaceable Ifland, animated by the fight of Hebe, did wonders, and was declared victor again? when Atimir, vexed to be a fpectator of his rival's glory, and flattered with the

thought

thought of receiving the prize from Hebe's hand, went
and presented himself at the end of the lists.

The two rivals looked on each other scornfully; and
that course between two such great princes was celebrated by the new trouble it caused the two princesses.
The princes ran one against the other with equal advantage, and broke their lances without any disorder. The
shouts of the spectators redoubled, and they without
giving their horses time to breathe, returned to take
fresh lances, and ran with the same success and address
as at first. The king, who feared lest fortune should declare one of them victors, sent presently to tell them,
that they ought to be satisfied with the glory they had
gained, and to desire them to put an end to the courses.

When the person the king sent, came up to them, they
heard him with a great deal of impatience, especially
Atimir; who taking upon him to speak, said, ' Go tell
.' the king, I should be unworthy of the honour he does
' me, in concerning himself with my glory, if I should
' suffer a conqueror.' ' Let us see then (said the prince
' of the Peaceable Island, spurring on his horse with
' great ardour,) which merits most the kings esteem,
' and the favours of fortune.

The messenger was not returned to the king, before
the two rivals, urged on by sentiments more prevalent
than the prize, began the course; wherein fortune fa-
voured the audacious Atimir, and pronounced him
victor; the prince of the Peaceable Island's horse,
wearied with the courses he had made, falling down,
and throwing his master on the sand: how great was
Atimir's joy, and that unfortunate prince's rage!
He got up quickly, and going up to his rival before any
came to them, ' You have overcome me in sports,
' Atimir, (said he, with an air sufficient to shew his
' passion;) but with my sword I will decide our dif-
' ferences.' ' I consent, (replied the fiery Atimir,)
' and will meet you to-morrow at sun-rise, in the wood,
'' at the end of the palace-gardens.' As they had made
an end of these words, the judges of the field came up
to them; whereupon they disguised their mutual rage,
lest the king should prevent their designs.

The

The prince of the Peaceable Iſland mounted his horſe again, and rid with all ſpeed to leave the fatal p'ace, where Atimir had vanquiſhed him. In the mean time that prince went to receive the prize of courſe from Hebe, who preſented it to him with a confuſion that diſcovered the different commotions of her ſoul; and Atimir, in taking it, committed all the extravagance of a man very much in love.

The king and queen, who had their eyes fixed on them, obſerving him all the time, and returned to their palace very much diſſatisfied with the ending of that day. Atimir, poſſeſſed with his paſſion, went out of the liſts without any attendants; and Ileria, outrageous with grief and jealouſy, went back to her apartments.

Various then were the thoughts of Hebe: ‘ I muſt ‘ go hence, (ſaid ſhe to herſelf,) ſince no other remedy ‘ can be found to prevent the misfortunes that I fore- ‘ ſee.’

At the ſame time the king and queen reſolved to deſire Atimir to go home, to avoid the new troubles his love might create; which ſame propoſition they likewiſe determined to make to the prince of the Peaceable Iſland, that neither party might take umbrage thereat But the princes haſty reſolutions prevented this prudent foreſight; for while they deliberated on their departure, the others prepared for the combat.

As ſoon as Hebe came back from the courſes, ſhe aſked for the prince, her ſpouſe, who they told her was in the gardens of the palace, very melancholy, and willing to be alone. The beautiful Hebe thought it her duty to go and comfort him after his ill-fortune; ſo, without ſtaying in her apartment; ſhe went into the gardens, followed by ſome of her women.

She was looking for the prince, when entering into a ſhady walk, ſhe eſpied the amorous Atimir, who tranſported with his paſſion, and regarding nothing elſe, fell on his knees ſome diſtance from the princeſs, and drawing the ſword he that day received from her. ‘ Hear ‘ me, charming Hebe, (ſaid he,) or let me die at your ‘ feet.’

The

The women, frightened at this action of the prince, threw themselves upon him, endeavouring to take away his sword, which he turned with great rage on the other side. Hebe, the unhappy Hebe, was for flying: but how great must our reason be, that can force us from what we love!

The desire of keeping this adventure a secret, with her design to entreat Atimir to strive to cure a passion so fatal to them both, and the compassion so moving an object created, all contributed to stay the princess, who made up to the prince; her presence suspended his fury; his sword he let fall at her feet, and never more trouble, love, and grief, appeared at once in so short a conversation.

Words are not tender enough to express what these two unhappy lovers then endured: Hebe, uneasy to see herself with Atimir, and so nigh the prince of the Peaceable Island, made a great effort on herself to leave him, charging him never to see her more. How cruel was this command! Had not Atimir called to mind the engagement he lay under to fight the prince of the Peaceable Island, he had a thousand times turned the sword upon himself; but alas! he chose rather to die, revenging himself on his rival.

The fair Hebe retired instantly to her apartment, the more securely to avoid the presence of Atimir: ' Merciless Fairy, (cried she,) you only told me of ' death, if ever I saw this unhappy prince; but now I ' feel torments a thousand times more grievous!' Then sending to seek for the prince in the gardens and the palace, and not finding him, her uneasiness increased; they sought him all the night to no purpose; for he hid himself in a hut in the midst of the wood, that he might not be prevented from meeting at the place appointed, which he repaired to at sun-rise, were Atimir arrived soon after. These two rivals, impatient to revenge themselves, and to gain the victory, drew their swords; which was the first time the prince of the Peaceable Island ever made use of his, since there never was any war in his dominions.

Nevertheless

6

Neverthelefs, he appeared not the lefs formidable enemy to Atimir; for though he had but little experience, he had courage, was in love, and fought like a man that defpifed death; while Atimir maintained the great reputation he had fo worthily gained.

Thefe two princes were animated by paffions too much different, not to render the end of this duel fatal, for after they had a long time maintained an equal advantage, they made too fuch furious thrufts at each other, that both fell on the grafs, which they died with their blood.

The prince of the Peaceable Ifland fainted away inftantly with the lofs of his; and Atimir, mortally wounded, pronounced the name of Hebe as he expired.

Some of thofe perfons who were fent to look for the prince of the Peaceable Ifland, arrived at that fatal place, and were feized with horror at fo difmal a fight.

The princefs Hebe, drawn by her difquiet, was going into the gardens, when hearing the fhrieks of people who pronounced confufedly the names of the two princes, fhe hereupon ran and found thofe fo fad and difmal objects: fhe thought that the prince her hufband was dead as well as Atimir, who at that time were both alike to her; when, after having looked fome time on thofe unhappy princes, fhe cried out dolefully, ' Ye ' precious lives, which were facrificed for me, I will re- ' venge you by the lofs of my own.' After thefe words fhe fell on the fatal fword Atimir received from her, and had pierced her breaft before the people (who were amazed at this cruel adventure) could hinder her.

Juft as fhe expired, the Fairy Anguiletta appeared, who, touched with fo many misfortunes which fhe had oppofed with all her power, accufed fate, and could not forbear fhedding tears. Then thinking of affifting the prince of the Peaceable Ifland, whom fhe knew was not dead, fhe cured him of his wounds, and tranfported him inftantly into his own ifle; where, by the wonderful gift fhe had beftowed on it, that prince was confoled for the lofs he had fuftained, and forgot his paffion for Hebe.

B.6. The

The king and queen, who had not the like affistance, gave themfelves up entirely to grief, which was only to be worn off by time. And as for Ileria, her defpair cannot be expreffed, who was always both faithful to her grief, and the ungrateful Atimir.

When Anguiletta had tranfported the prince of the Peaceable Ifland into his own dominions, fhe touched with her wand the unfortunate remains of the lovely Atimir and the beautiful Hebe, who in an inftant were changed into two trees of an admirable beauty, which the Fairy named *Charms*, to preferve for ever the remembrance of thofe which fhone fo bright in thefe unhappy lovers.

———————

THE

ROYAL RAM;

OR, THE

WISHES.

IN thofe happy days when Fairies were common, there lived a king who had three beautiful young daughters, who were all deferving; but the youngeft whofe name was Miranda, being the moft amiable, and her father's favourite, was allowed as many clothes in a month, as her fifters had in a year; but fhe being fo generous as to let them partake with her, it made no difference amongft them.

The king having had neighbours, who, tired with a long peace, obliged him to raife an army, and to take the field, left his daughters with a governante in a caftle,

where they might hear news from him every day; and
when he had subdued his enemies, and drove them out of
his dominions, came to the castle to see his Miranda, whom
he doated on. The three princesses bespoke themselves
every one a robe of sattin; the eldest's was green,
adorned with emeralds; the second's was blue, set off
with turquoises; and the younge's white, bedecked
with diamonds. And in these dresses they went to
meet the king, and to congratulate him on his victories.

When he saw them so beautiful and gay, he embraced
them all tenderly, but especially Miranda. After a
magnificent entertainment that was served up, the king,
who loved to draw consequences from the most trivial
matters, asked the eldest, why she put on a green gown?
' Sir, (said she,) after hearing of your great deeds, I
' thought green might express my joy, and the hopes of
' your return.' ' That's very well, (said the king.)
' And you, daughter, (continued he to the second,) how
' came you to put on a blue gown? ' To shew, sir,
' (said she,) we ought to implore the gods in your fa-
' vour; and that in seeing you, I behold the heavens and
' the brightest stars.' ' Now, (said the king,) you
' speak like an oracle. And you, Miranda, (said the
' king,) what made you dress yourself in white?'
' Because, (said she,) it becomes me better than any
' other colour:' How, (said the king, a little angrily,)
' was that only your design?' ' I had that of pleasing
' you, (said the princess,) and I think I need no other.'
Whereupon the king was mightily pleased at her
turn of thought, and said, That since he had eaten a
pretty deal at supper, he would not go to bed so soon,
therefore he would have them tell him their dreams the
night before his return.

The eldest said, she dreamed he brought her a gown,
the gold and jewels of which were brighter than the sun;
the second said, she dreamed that he brought her a
golden spining-wheel and distaff, for her to spin herself
some shifts; and the youngest said, she dreamed he
married her second sister off, and, on the wedding-day,
held a golden ewer, and said, ' Come Miranda, come
' and wash you.'

The

The king, who was angry at this dream, knit his brow, made a thousand wry faces, and went into his chamber, where throwing himself upon his bed, he could not forget his daughter's dream : ‘ This insolent baggage, (said he,) would make me her domestic slave ; ‘ I am not amazed now, why she put on a white gown ‘ with thinking of me ; she looks on me as one unworthy ‘ of her reflections ; but I'll prevent her ill designs.’ Hereupon he got up in a rage ; and though it was not yet day, he sent for the captain of his guards, and said to him ; ‘ You have heard of Miranda's dream, which ‘ forebodes some treason ; therefore I would have you ‘ take her presently, and carry her into the forest and ‘ kill her, and afterwards bring me her heart and ‘ tongue : If you deceive me, I'll put you to the most ‘ cruel death I can think of.’ The captain of the guards was very much surprised at so barbarous an order, but durst not seem averse to it, lest the king should take away his commission, but promised him to perform it. Then going to the princess's chamber, which he had much ado to get to, it being so very early, he told her, the king had sent him for her. Whereupon she rose presently : a little Moor, that she called Patpatay, held up her train, and her young ape, named Grabugeon, and a little dog, which she called Tintin, ran by her side.

The captain of the guard carried her into the garden, telling her the king was taking a little fresh air ; and then pretending to look for him, and not finding him, told her, he was without dispute gone from thence into the forest. Then opening the little door that led into the forest, and day coming on, the princess observed that her conductor shed some tears, and seemed melancholy ; whereupon she said to him, with an air of sweetness, ‘ What is the matter, you seem so much afflicted ?’ ‘ Alas ! madam, (cried he) who can be otherwise ? The ‘ king has ordered me to kill you here, and to carry ‘ him your heart and tongue, or else he will put me to ‘ death.’ At these words the poor princess turned pale, and fell a crying, and in that condition looked like a

lamb

lamb that was going to the slaughter; then fixing her eyes on the captain, without any anger, said to him, ' Have you courage enough to kill me, who never did ' you any injury in my life, but rather always spoke to ' the king in your favour? But if I have deserved my ' father's anger, I submit without murmuring. Alas! ' I have shew him but too much love and respect, for ' him to complain without injustice.' ' Fear not fair ' princess, (said the officer) I'll sooner suffer the death ' I am threatened with, than be guilty of so barbarous ' an action; but when I am gone you will not be more ' safe: we must find out some expedient to persuade ' the king you are dead.'

' What way can we find out? (replied Miranda.) ' He will not be satisfied, unless he sees my tongue and ' heart. At that Patypata, who stood by and heard all, without being observed by either the princess or the captain, advanced boldly, and throwing herself at Miranda's feet, said, ' I come, madam, to offer you ' my life, let me be the sacrifice: I shall be but too well ' pleased to die for so good a mistress.' ' I have no ' need of so tender a proof of thy friendship, (said the ' princess, kissing her) thy life ought now to be as dear ' to me as my own. Whereupon Grabugeon came forward, and said, ' You are in the right, my princess, to ' love so faithful a slave as Patypata; she may be more ' serviceable to you than I can, therefore I offer you ' my heart and tongue with joy.' ' Oh my pretty ' Grabugeon, (replied Miranda,) I cannot bear the thoughts of taking thy life away.' With that Tintin cry'd out, that it was insupportable to so faithful a dog as he was, that any other but him should lay down their life for his mistress; and thereupon arose a great dispute between Patypata, Grabugeon, and Tinto: in short, Grabugeon being quicker than the rest, clim'd up to the top of a high tree, and threw himself down, and broke his neck; and the Captain of the Guard, with a great deal of persuasion, got leave of the princess to cut out his tongue; but it proved too small to venture to cheat the king with it.

' Alas!'

'Alas! my poor little ape, said the princess, thou haft
'loft thy life without doing me any fervice! That
'honour is reserved for me, interrupted the Moor;'
and at the fame time cut her throat with the knife that
Grabugeon's tongue was cut out with. The officer
was for carrying her tongue, but that it was too black
to pass for Myranda's 'How unfortunate am I, (said
'the princess, weeping,) thus to lose what I love, and
'not to be one whit the better for it.' 'If you had
'accepted of my propofition, faid Tintin, you would
'have none to have griev'd for but me, and I fhould
'have had the fatisfaction of being regretted alone.'
Whereupon Miranda kifs'd her little dog, and griev'd
fo much, that fhe fwoon'd away, and when fhe came to
herfelf found her dog dead, her conductor gone, and
herfelf l ft with her three dead favourites: which fhe
buried in a hole that was ready dug hard by a tree, and
then bethought herfelf of her own fecurity.

As the foreft was not far from her father's court, it
was not fafe for her to ftay there long, left fhe fhould be
know by fome of the paffengers, therefore fhe made all
the hafte fhe could to get out of it: but the foreft was
fo large, and the fun fo hot, that fhe was ready to die
-with heat, fear, and wearinefs; and was in continual
apprehenfions left her father fhould follow and kill her:
-but ftill continued going forwards, making lamentable
complaints, having her gown almoft torn off, and her
fkin fcratched by the thorns and brambles At laft
hearing the bleating of fheep. 'Without doubt, (faid
'fhe to herfelf,) here are fome fhepherds with the flocks,
'who may direct me to fome hamlet where I may
'difguife myfelf in fome country drefs: for alas! con-
'tinued fhe, princes are not always the moft happy:
'who believes that I am a run-away? that my father,
'without any caufe or reafon, feeks my life? and that
'I, to fave it, muft be forced to difguife myfelf?'
While fhe was making thefe reflections, fhe arrived at
the place from whence fhe heard the bleating; but
how great was her furprife, when fhe came to a fpacious
plain, to fee a large Ram, as white as fnow; his horns
                                                    were

were gilt, a garland of flowers faſtened about his neck,
his legs were adorned with bracelets of pearls of a prodigious ſize, and he was laid on orange flowers, and
ſhaded from the heat of the ſun by a pavilion of cloth
of gold. An hundred ſheep finely adorned were waiting about him, ſome drinking coffee, ſherbet, and le-
monade; others eating ſtrawberries and cream, and
ſweetmeats; and others again playing at laſquenet and
baſſet; ſome had rich collars of gold, with a gallant device, and ſome had their ears bored, and full of ribbons,
Miranda was ſo much amazed, that ſhe was perfectly
motionleſs, and looked about for the ſhepherd of ſuch
an extraordinary flock, when the beautiful ram came
bounding and ſkipping, and ſaid, ‘ Approach, divine
‘ princeſs, be not afraid of ſuch gentle pacific creatures
‘ as we are.’ ‘ What prodigy is it (ſaid the princeſs,
‘ ſtepping back) to hear ſheep ſpeak?’ ‘ Alas! madam,
‘ (ſaid the ram) your ape and dog ſpoke, and why is
‘ it more ſtrange that we ſhould?’ ‘ A fairy (anſwered
‘ Miranda) beſtowed that gift upon them ’ ‘ And
‘ might not the like adventure attend us? (replied the
‘ ram, ſmiling:) but my princeſs what brought you
‘ hither?’ ‘ A thouſand misfortunes, (replied Miranda)
‘ I am the moſt miſerable perſon in the world, and
‘ ſeek an aſylum to avoid the rage of a father.’ ‘ Come,
‘ madam, with me (replied the ram) I will afford you
‘ one, where you ſhall be known by none, and be ab-
‘ ſolute miſtreſs.’ ‘ But I am not able to follow you,
‘ (replied ſhe) I am ſo weary.’ Whereupon the ram
ordered his chariot, and ſoon after appeared ſix goats,
harneſſed to a gourd ſhell, large enough for two perſons
to ſit in with eaſe, and lined with valvet. The princeſs
placed herſelf in it, admiring an equipage ſo novel, and
the ram got in after her, and then drove to the cavern's
mouth, which was ſtopped by a large ſtone, which, on
the ram's touching with his foot, removed. After
which, he told the princeſs ſhe might go done without
danger; which ſhe would hardly have ever conſented
to, had not her fear of being taken prompted her to it;
and upon that account, ſhe never heſitated, but followed
her conductor.

As

As the steps were very numerous, the princess thought that she was either going to pay a visit to their antipodes, or the Elysian shades; but was much more surprised when she discovered a vast plain, enamelled with various flowers, which excelled all the perfumes she had ever smelt, surrounded with a large river of orange flower water. In the midst of this plain were fountains of wine, rosa-solis, and other exquisite liquors, which formed cascades and other pleasant purling brooks, and here and there holts of trees, which served for shelter to a variety of choice birds and fowls, as partridges, quails, pheasants, ortolans, turkeys, pullets, &c. and in some parts, the air was darkened with showers of biscuits, blanched almonds, tarts, cheesecakes, marrow-puddings, and all manner of sweetmeats, both wet and dry; and in short, with all necessaries of life, with great plenty of crown-pieces, guineas, pearls, and diamonds. Without doubt, the rarity and usefulness of this rain would have brought the Royal Ram a great many visitors, if he had been desirous of company; but all the writers that mention him, assure us, that he chose to be retired, and was as grave as any Roman senator.

As it was the pleasantest season of the year when Miranda arrived there, she saw no other palace than what chambers, halls, closets, orange-trees, sessamine, honey-suckles, and rose-trees formed by intermixing their boughs. The princely ram told Miranda, that he had reigned sovereign there several years, and had sufficient cause to be afflicted; but that he refrained from tears, that he might not remind her of her misfortunes. ' Your manner of treatment, charming ' sheep, (said she) is somewhat so generous, that I can- ' not express my acknowledgement enough; that I ' must confess, that what I see seems so extraordinary, ' I know not what to think of it.' No sooner had she pronounced these words, but there appeared a troop of beautiful nymphs, who presented her with fruit out of amber baskets; but when she went near them, they insensibly moved from her; and at last reaching out her hand to take hold of one of them, she soon perceived
                                                                    they

they were only fantoms. ' Alas! (faid fhe, weeping)
' where am I, and what are thefe?' At that inftant
the Royal Ram, for fo I muft call him, returning,
having left her fome moments, and feeing her fhed
tears, remained motionlefs, and ready to die at her
feet.

' What is the matter with my beautiful princefs?
' (faid he) have I any way failed in the refpect that
' is due to you?, ' No, (faid fhe) but I am not
' ufed to live among the dead, and with fheep that
talk: every thing here terrifies me; and though my
' obligation is great to you for bringing me hither, yet
' I muft beg one favour more of you, to conduct me
' back.' ' Fright not yourfelf, (replied he) vouchfafe
' to hear me quietly, and you fhall know my deplor-
' able adventure.'

' I was born a prince: a great race of kings, who
' were my anceftors, left me in poffeffion of one of
' the moft beautiful kingdoms in the world; my fub-
' jects loved me, my neighbours both fear'd and envy'd
' me, and I was efteem'd with fome juftice. My per-
' fon was not indifferent to thofe that faw me; and
' being a great lover of hunting, and as I was one day
' purfuing a ftag, and feparated from my attendants,
' the ftag took into a pond: I plunged my horfe in
' after him with too much imprudence, as well as rafh-
' nefs; but, inftead of finding the water cold, I found
' it extraordinary hot, and the pond becoming dry all
' on a fudden, there iffued out of a cliff a terrible fire,
' and I fell to the bottom from off the precipice, where
' I could fee nothing but flames. I believed myfelf
' loft, when I heard a voice fay, They muft be greater
' flames that warm thy heart, ungrateful man. Alas!
' cried I, who is that who complains of my coolnefs?
' An unfortunate wretch, replied the voice, who adores
' you without hope. At the fame time the fire went
' out, and I faw a fairy, whom I knew from my youth,
' and whofe age and uglinefs always frightened me;
' fhe was leaning on a young flave of incomparable
' beauty, who was loaded with chains of gold, to denote
                                        ' her

' her flavery. What prodigy is this, faid I to Ragotte,
' which was the fairy's name; was this done by your
' orders? Alas! by whofe orders elfe do you think?
' replied fhe? Have you never known my fentiments
' till now? Muft I be forced to explain myfelf—my
' eyes ufed never to fail of conquefts; have they now
' loft all their power? Confider how low I ftoop, 'tis a
' fairy that makes this confeffion, and kings are, in
' refpect to them, but as ants. I am entirely at your
' pleafure, faid I to her, with an air and tone that ex-
' preffed fome impatience; but what is it that you afk?
' Is it my crown, my cities, or my treafure? Oh wretch,
' replied fhe, difdainfully, I can make my fkullions,
' when I pleafe, greater than thee: I afk thy heart; my
' eyes have afked it a thoufand times, and thou haft
' not underftood them, or at leaft wouldft not. Wert
' though engaged with any other, I fhould not interrupt
' thee in thy amours; but I have too great an intereft
' in thee not to difcover the indifference of thy heart.
' Ah! grant me thy love, added fhe, fhutting her
' mouth, to render it the more agreeable, and rolling
' her eyes about, I will be thy dear Ragotte, will add
' twenty kingdoms to that you poffefs, an hundred
' towers of gold, five hundred full of filver, and what-
' ever thou canft defire befides.

' Madam Ragotte, faid I to her, I beg of you, by all
' the charms that render you lovely, to fet me at liber-
' ty, and then we'll fee what I can do to pleafe you.
' Oh traitor! cried fhe, if thou loveft me, thou wouldft
' not mourn fo much after thy own kingdom; but
' be content to live in a grotto, wood, or defert. Do
' not believe me to be fo great a novice; thou thinkeft
' of ftealing away, but I tell you for your comfort,
' you muft ftay here; and the firft thing you fhall do,
' fhall be to keep my fheep, which have as much wit,
' and fpeak as well as though doft. At the fame time
' fhe brought me into this plain, where we are now,
' and fhewed me her flock, which I looked on but little;
' for that beautiful flave that was with her took up all
' my regard, and my eyes betrayed me; which the

' cruel Ragotte obferving, flew upon her, and ftabb'd
' her in the eye with her bodkin, and fo deprived that
' adorable object of her life. At this difmal fight, I fell
' on Ragotte, and clapping my hand upon my fword,
' was going to facrifice her to the manes of that dear
' flave, had fhe not rendered me motionlefs by her art.
' My effort being vain, I fell on the ground, and en-
' deavoured to kill myfelf, to deliver myfelf from that
' wretched ftate I was reduced to; when fhe, with an
' ironical fmile, faid to me, I will make you feel my
' power; you are at prefent a lion, but fhall, ere long,
' be a fheep. Whereupon touching me with her wand,
' I found myfelf metamorphofed, fuch as you fee me:
' but retained both my fpeech, and thofe fentiments of
' grief which I owe to my unhappy ftate. Thou fhalt
' be five years a fheep, (continued fhe) and abfolute
' mafter of this fweet abode: while I, feparate from
' thee, and never beholding thy agreeable form, fhall
' think on nothing but the hatred I bear thee.' Hereupon fhe difappeared; and if any thing could have foftened my misfortunes, or given any allay to my dif-
grace, 'twas her abfence.

The fheep fhe fpoke of acknowledged me to be their
king, told me all their misfortunes, how they difpleafed
the fairy, how fhe had compofed a flock of them, and that
they all underwent the fame punifhment. But (added
he) when their time is expired, they will refume their
own forms, and leave the flock; and for thofe who are
Rigotta's rivals, or enemies, whom fhe has killed, they
abide here an age before they return into the world
again: of which number the young flave is, whom I
told you of. I have feen her feveral months together,
but fhe never fpeaks to me; and, when I approach'd
towards her, it grieved me when I knew it was only a
fhadow: but having obferved one of my flock always by
that phantom, I underftood he was her lover, whom
Ragotte, jealous of the tender impreffions they had
made on each other, had taken from her.

This was the reafon that made me remove from that
fairy, and for thefe laft three years, think of nothing
but

but my liberty, which was what engaged me so often to the forest, where I sometimes have seen you, fair princess, driving your chaise, like Diana, in her silver chariot, and at other times mounted on a fiery steed, riding over the plains with the princesses and ladies of the court, and like another, always sure to gain the prize. Alas! if at those times I durst have spoke, what fine things should I have said, when my heart offered up its secret vows? But how would you have received the declaration of an unhappy sheep like me.

Miranda was so much concerned at what she heard, that she hardly knew what answer to make; however, paying him some civilities, which gave him some hopes, she told him, she should not be so much afraid of those shades, since they were to come to life again: ‘ But ‘ alas! continued she) if my poor Patypata, my dear ‘ Grabugeon, and my pretty Tintin, who died to serve ‘ me, were to meet with the like fate, I should not be so ‘ much concerned here.’

Tho’ the Royal Ram underwent great disgraces, yet had he a great many admirable privileges, ‘ Go, ‘ (said he) to his first ’squire, who was a sheep of a good ‘ mein, go fetch the Moor, the monkey, and the little ‘ Dog; their shades may divert our princess.’ Soon after Miranda saw them; and though they came not nigh enough to be touched by her, yet their presence was some comfort to her. In short the Royal Ram, who was endued with all the wit and delicacy proper to support an agreeable conversation, was so passionately in love with Miranda, that she began to have some regard for him, and to make some returns; for what can be displeasing in a beautiful, kind, caressing sheep, especially when known to be a king, whose metamorphosis was to have an end? Thus the princess passed her days in the sweet expectation of a more happy fate, while the gallant Ram, whose thoughts were soley bent on her, made entertainments, concerts of music; and did every thing that was in his power to divert her; his troop assisted him in them, and the shades contributing somewhat thereunto.

One

One evening, when the couriers arrived, for he was very fond of news, and always had the beft, they told him, that the eldeft fifter of the princefs Miranda, was going to marry a great prince, and that the nuptials were to be very magnificent. ' Alas! (cried the young ' princefs) how unfortunate am I, not to fee fuch fine ' things? I am here under ground with ghofts and fheep, ' while my fifter, who will be dreffed as fine as a queen, ' will have all the court made to her, and I fhall be the ' only one who fhall not partake of her joy.' ' Madam, ' why do you complain? (faid the Royal Ram to her) ' Have I denied your going to the wedding! Go, when ' you pleafe; but give me your word, you will come ' again: if you deny me this, you fhall fee me expire ' at your feet; for my love is too violent for me to ' fupport myfelf when I fhall lofe you.' Miranda pro- mifed him nothing fhould prevent her return. He gave her an equipage fuitable to her birth: fhe was dreffed very richly, and neglected nothing that might fet off her charms; fhe got into a chariot of mother of pearl, drawn by fix creatures that were half griffins, and newly arrived from the antipodes, and was attended by a great number of officers that were richly dreffed, and who had been fent a great way to make up her train.

With this equipage fhe arrived at the king her father's court, juft when they were celebrating the marriage; as foon as fhe entered, fhe furprifed all that faw her with the luftre of her beauty and jewels, and heard nothing but acclamations in her own praife. The king looking at her with great attention and pleafure, which put her into fome fear left he fhould know her; but he was fo much prepoffeffed with her death, that he had not the leaft idea of her. Neverthelefs, the apprehenfions of being ftopped, prevented her ftaying 'till the ceremony was over, and made her go away fuddenly, leaving a box of jewels behind her, whereupon thefe words were written, Thefe Jewels are for the new-married couple: and when they opened it, there was nothing in it. The king, who had flattered himfelf with fome hopes, and was defirous to know who fhe was, was in the ut-

moft

most despair when he knew she was gone, and ordered
his officer, whenever she came again, to shut the gates
and keep her in. Though Miranda was not long ab-
sent, yet it seemed an age to the Royal Ram, who waited
for her by a fountain side in the thickest of the forest,
where he had brought out immense riches to offer her
as an acknowledgement of her return. As soon as he
saw her, he ran towards her, skipping and bounding,
caressing her in this manner a thousand times, laid
down at her feet, kissed her hand, told her is disquiets
and impatience; wherein his passion afforded him so
much eloquence, that the princess was charmed with
it.

Some time afterwards the king married his second
daughter, and Miranda being informed of it, desired
the Ram to let her go again; who at that proposition, was
extremely grieved; a secret foresight prepossessed him
with his misfortune; but as it is not always in our
power to prevent what we foresee, so his complaisancy
to the princess overbalancing his interest in her, he was
not able to deny her. ' You will leave me, Madam,
' (said he) but this proceeds more from my ill fortune
' than from you; I consent to your desires, since I
' never could make you a greater sacrifice.' She assured
him she would stay no longer than she had done before:
and she would be as much concerned as himself to be
detained; and desired him not to make himself uneasy.
In short, she had the same equipage as before, and arrived t ere just as the ceremony began. Her presence,
notwithstanding their attention to the ceremony, occa-
sioned a general shout of joy and admiration, and drew
the eyes of all the princes upon her; who found her
beauty so extraordinary and uncommon, that they could
hardly believe her to be mortal. The king was overjoyed to see her again, and never took his eyes off from
her but once, to give orders to lock up all the gates.
When the ceremony was almost over, the princess got
up suddenly to steal out of the crowd, but was very
much surprised and vexed to find all the gates shut.

The king went up to her with great respect, and a
submis- .

fubmiſſion that gave her ſome encouragement, deſiring her not to deprive him ſo ſoon of the pleaſure of ſeeing her, and to honour him at his court with her preſence. Then leading her into a magnificent hall, where all the court was, he himſelf held a golden baſon full of water for her to waſh her hands in. At this the princeſs, who was no longer miſtreſs of her tranſport, threw herſelf at his feet; and embracing his knees, ſaid, ' See, ſir, ' my dream is fulfilled; you have held a baſon for me ' to waſh in, the day of my ſiſter's wedding, without ' any misfortune attending, you.'

The king ſoon knew her to be his daughter Miranda, and embracing her, and ſhedding ſome tears, ſaid, ' Alas! my dear child, can you forget the cruelty of a ' father, who would have ſacrificed your life, becauſe ' he thought your dream denoted the loſs of his crown? ' It ſhall be ſo, (continued he) ſince both your ſiſters ' are married, and have each a crown, mine ſhall be ' your's.' And at that inſtant riſing up, he put the crown on the princeſs's head, and then ſaid, ' The gods ' preſerve the queen Miranda.' Whereupon the whole court gave a great ſhout of joy, and her two ſiſters came and hung about her neck, and embraced her a thouſand times. Miranda was ſo much overjoyed, that ſhe both cried and laughed, embraced one and talked to another, thanked the king, and aſked for the captain of the guards, to whom ſhe was obliged for all; and being told that he was dead, was very much grieved thereat. When they were at the table, the king deſired to hear what had happened to her from the day whereon thoſe fatal orders were given; which ſhe acquieſcing with, related her whole ſtory, without omitting the leaſt circumſtance. But while ſhe was thus engaged with the king and her ſiſters, the time of her return was elapſed, and the amorous Ram became ſo uneaſy, that he was no longer maſter of himſelf, and ſeeing that ſhe came not again, ſaid to himſelf, ' My unhappy form of a ſheep is dif- ' pleaſing to her; alas! too unfortunate lover, what ' ſhall I do without Miranda; Ragotte, inhuman fairy, ' how great is thy revenge, for my indifference towards

C   ' thee

thee.' Complaining in this manner, and feeing night approaching, without any appearance of his princefs's coming, he ran to the palace and afked for Miranda; but as every body had heard of his adventure, and were unwilling that the princefs fhould go back again with him, they refufed him the fight of her in fo rude a manner, that he fetched fighs, and made complaints capable of piercing the hearts of all that heard him, except the foldiers that kept the gates; and at laft, overcome with his grief, laid himfelf down and died.

The king, who knew nothing of this deep tragedy, propofed to his daughter to ride in a chariot through all the ftreets in the city, to fhew her to her fubjects; but what a difmal fight was it to her, when they got out of the gates of the palace, to fee her dear fheep ftretched on the ground void of life? She jumped with precipitation out of the chariot, ran to him, cried over him, and bemoaned the death of the Royal Ram, which fhe knew was owing to her not being fo good as her word, and in her defpair thought to have partook of his fate.

The fairy Lauretina, who had prefided over their births, fenfibly affected at the lovers' unfortunate fituation, came to their relief, and with a touch of her talifman, not only reftored the Royal Ram to life, but to his natural form as a beautiful prince. The good old king, happy in his wifhes for his daughter, finding the prince royally defcended, confented to their union; and in full court made them heirs to his kingdom.

Thus we fee by virtue and perfeverance, though calamities may furround us.—Yet if we are good, we fhall ultimately be happy.

GRACIOSA

AND

PERCINET.

THERE was a king and queen who had only one daughter. Her beauty, her sweetness of temper, and her wit, which were incomparable, caused her parents to give her the name of Graciofa. She was her mother's sole delight; who ordered new garments for her every morning throughout the year, either of cloth of gold, velvet or fattin. Yet though she was dreffed in the richeft manner, she was not proud, nor vain-glorious. She fpent the morning with learned perfons, who taught her all manner of fciences; and in the afternoon she was employed at her needle, in company with the queen. At dinner and fupper she was ferved in plate, and the table was fpread with difhes of fweetmeats, and all manner of confectionary: fo that she was faid to be the moft happy princefs in the world.

There was in the fame court an old maid, but very rich, called the dutchefs Grognon, every way a moft frightful creature to look upon; her hair was red as fire; she had a face dreadfully broad, and covered over with large pimples; of both her eyes that formerly she had, there nothing remained but continual b'ear; her mouth was fo wide as if she would have devoured all the world; only thofe fears ceafed, when people faw she had no teeth: she was hunch-back'd and crump fhou'der'd both before and behind, and lame of both legs. This fort of mon-

fters

sters bear a great malice to all those that are lovely and beautiful. She mortally hated Graciosa upon this account, and retired from court that she might not hear the continual praises bestowed on her charms. She lived in a particular castle of her own, not far distant; and when any person who came to visit her, spoke in praise of the princess, she would cry out in a violent passion, 'tis false, 'tis false; she is not a bit handsome; I have more charms in my little finger than she has in her whole body.

In the mean time the queen fell sick and died, and the princess Graciosa was very near following her, such was her grief for the loss of so good a mother. The king also no less bemoan'd his fatal divorce from so dear and loving a wife; he shut himself up in his palace for a whole year together; till at length his physicians, fearing lest he should impair his health, besought him for his own good to take the air, and divert himself. In compliance with this advice, he one day went a hunting, but the weather being extremely hot, and perceiving a fair castle not far off, upon the purlieus of the forest, thither he made with all his train, and went to repose himself.

Immediately the dutchess Grognon, having notice of the king's arrival, (for to her it was that the castle belonged) made haste to receive him, and told him that the coolest part of the castle was a large handsome underroom, to which she desired his majesty would give her leave to conduct him. Accordingly the king went along with her, and seeing in the room about two hundred pipes all in rows one above another, he asked her whether it were for her own use only that she made such large provision. ' Yes, sir, (said she,) I provide for ' none but myself and family; I should be very glad if ' your majesty would' be pleased to taste my liquors; ' here is Canary, St. Laurent, Champaigne, Hermitage, ' Rivesalte, Rosa solas, Persicot, Fenouillet; which ' will your majesty make choice of?' ' Frankly, (said ' the king,) I hold your Champaigne wine to be the ' best.' Grognon immediately took a little hammer, and

and having given a rap or two at the head of the pipe,
it opened, and out came a million of piftoles: ha!
what's the meaning of this, faid fhe, with a fmile! and
knocking at the head of another pipe, out flew as many
double louis d'ors as would have filled a bufhel. Good
God! what's all this for, faid fhe, in a feign'd aftonifh-
men!! From thence paffed to the third, fhe knocked in
the fame manner, and there iffued as many pearls and
diamonds as covered the floor. ' Well, fir, (faid fhe
' to the king,) this is paft my underftanding; fome
' body muft certainly have robbed me of my fine wines,
' and filled up the veffels with thefe trifles.' ' Trifles!
' (cried the king in amazement) in the name of pro-
' phecy, madam Grognon, do you call thefe trifles?
' Why, woman, thefe trifles are enough to buy ten
' cities as big as London.' ' Well then, fir (faid fhe) to
' be plain with you, all thefe pipes are full of gold and
' precious ftones, and I will make you mafter of them
' upon condition that you will marry me.' ' A match,
' (cried the king who loved money better than any
' thing) this very day, if you pleafe, before we ftir out
' of the caftle. But ftay (faid fhe) there is one condi-
' tion more: I will be miftrefs of your daughter as her
' mother was: fhe fhall be wholly at my command,
' you fhall leave me the fole difpofal of her.' ' Agreed,
' (cried the king) you fhall be miftrefs of my daughter
' too: here is my hand upon it.' Grognon gave him
her hand: after which, having given him the key of
the wealthy cellar, they took their leaves.

So foon as the king arrived at his palace, Graciofa
hearing that her father was returned, ran to meet him;
embraced him, and afked him whether he had had
good fport; to which her father replied, ' I have caught
' a pigeon alive.' ' Oh, fir, (faid fhe,) give it to me,
' and I will make it my care.' ' That cannot be, (con-
' tinued the king) for that I may more intelligibly
' explain myfelf, I muft tell thee, that I have met the
' dutchefs of Grognon, and taken her to be my wife.'
' Good heavens! (cried Graciofa, in her firft tranfports)
' do you call her a pigeon, who is ten thoufand times
C 3 ' uglier

' uglier than an owl?'——' Hold your tongue, (faid the
' king, fhewing himfelf fomewhat offended)——'Tis
' my pleafure that you love and refpect her as much
' as if fhe were your mother.——Go therefore and
' drefs yourfelf——for I intend this day to return back
' and meet her.

The princefs was very obedient; and went to her
chamber to drefs: but her nurfe, perceiving by her
eyes, that fomething troubled her, ' What is the mat-
' ter, my dear jewel, (faid fhe) why weeps my child?'
' Oh! my poor nurfe, (replied Graciofa) how is it
' poffible I fhould otherwife than weep, my father is
' going to bring me home a mother-in-law; and to com-
' complete my mifery, the only and moft cruel enemy
' I have in the world; in a word, it is the hideous
' Grognon.' How is it poffible to behold her within
' thefe curtains, which the queen, my dear mother, fo
' curioufly embroidered with her own hands? How is
' it poffible to carefs a hideous face that has fo impa-
' tiently fought my death?' ' My dear child, (replied
' the nurfe) there is a neceffity that your demeanor
' fhould be as confpicuoufly good, as your birth is great:
' princeffes, like yourfelf, ought to give greater exam-
' ple than others: and what more noble example can
' you give, than that of obedience to your father? Pro-
' mife me then, that you will not let Grognon fee you
' difcontented.' The princefs had much ado to refolve;
but the difcreet nurfe gave her fo many good reafons
for it, that fhe promifed at laft to put as good a face
upon the matter as fhe could, and comply with her ftep-
dame's humour.

Prefently fhe dreffed herfelf in a green garment, the
ground of which was cloth of gold: her white defhevelled
hair flowed in loofe ringlets about her fhoulders, the
fport of the playing and enamoured zephyrs, which was
the mode of that time; and fhe put on her head a light
garland of rofes and jeffamines, the leaves of which were
all of emeralds. In this drefs, Venus, the mother of
Cupid, would not have appeared fo fair. Yet her fad-
nefs, which fhe could not overcome, was ftill vifible in
her countenance.

But

But to return to Grognon: that hideous creature too was employed in the decoration of her deformity, she had caufed one fhoe to be made half a cubit higher than the other, to avoid limping as much as poffible fhe could. The valley on one fide of her back was filled up with a bolfter well ftuffed, to make it level with the mountain on the other fide: fhe had fupplied one of the empty holes with a glafs eye, the beft fhe could meet with; and had painted her cheeks white, and dyed her abominable carrots black; then fhe put on a purple robe lined with blue, over which fhe wore a yellow loofe veft tied with violet ribbons. And fhe would needs make her entry on horfeback, becaufe fhe had heard the queens of Spain were wont fo to do.

While the king was giving out his orders, Graciofa, who waited for his going to meet Grognon, went down into the garden, and walking forward into a gloomy grove, feated herfelf upon a bank of turfs: ' Here, ' (faid fhe) at length I am at liberty: here I may weep ' as long as I will without moleftation:' and with that fhe fell a fighing and weeping to that degree, that her eyes looked like two fountains of water. In this condition, having forgot all thoughts of returning again to the palace, fhe fpy'd coming towards her a page clad in green fattin, with white plumes in his cap, and the moft beautiful countenance in the world; who, when he drew near her, with one knee upon the ground; ' Princefs, (faid he) the king ftays for you.' She was furprifed by the attractive features which fhe obferved in the young page; and in regard fhe knew him not, thought he might be one of Grognon's train. ' How long (faid ' fhe) have you been admitted by the king into the ' number of his pages?' ' I belong not, madam, to the ' king, (faid he) I belong to you, and never will belong ' to any other.' ' You belong to me! (replied the ' princefs, full of aftonifhment) how is that poffible, fince ' I know not who you are!' ' Oh, princefs, (faid he) ' I never durft as yet attempt to make myfelf known. ' But the misfortunes with which you are threatned by ' the king's marriage, obliged me to fpeak to you fooner

C 4

' than otherwife I would have done. I had refolved to
' leave to time and my own affiduous fervices, the care
' of manifefting my love and refpect for your highnefs,
' and ——How! a page (cried the princefs) has a page
' the prefumption to tell me he loves me! This com-
' pleats the meafure of my misfortunes.' ' Fright not
' yourfelf, fair Graciofa, (faid the page, with a tender
' and refpectful air) I am Parcinet, a prince too well
' known, both by my birth, riches and learning, for you
' to find fo great an inequality between us, though your
' merit and beauty do indeed make a diftinction. I am
' often in thofe places which you frequent, though
' you fee me not. The gift of Faryifm, which I re-
' ceived from my birth, has greatly affifted to procure
' me the pleafure of your company; I will attend you
' this day, wherever you go, and perhaps it may fo fall
' out, that I may not prove a ufelefs companion.' All
the while he was fpeaking, the princefs looked upon him
with aftonifhment from which fhe could fcarce recover
herfelf. At laft, faid fhe, ' Are you the charming Per-
' cinet, whom I have fo great a defire to fee, and of whom
' fuch wonders are reported? How glad am I that you
' will be in the number of my friends! Now I no
' longer fear the mifchievous Grognon, fince you are fo
' kind to take me under your protection.' Some few
words more they had together, and then Graciofa returned to the palace, where fhe found a horfe ready har-
neffed and comparifoned, which Percinet had put into the
ftable, and which the grooms believed to be appointed
for her. She mounted immediately; for fhe was very
nimble and active, and the page took the horfe by the
bridle and led him, turning continually towards his
miftrefs, that he might have the pleafure of beholding
her.

When the horfe that was made choice of to carry Grognon, appeared near Graciofa's Palfry, you would on the
comparifon have thought him fome draught-horfe, taken
from a cart, and the furniture of the princefs's horfe
did fo glitter with precious ftones, that there was no
comparifon between them: of which the king, whofe
but

head was full of a thoufand other fancies, took no notice. But the eyes of all the lords and ladies were fixed only upon the princefs, whofe beauty they admired; and her pretty page in green, who they thought the moft genteel that belonged to the court.

They met Grognon upon the road in an open calafh, frightfully deformed and mifhaped, notwithftanding her arts to conceal it. The king and the princefs embraced her, and prefented her her horfe to get up and ride. But, perceiving Graciofa's Palfry, ' How (faid fhe) fhall ' that pufs have a finer horfe than I? I had rather ' never be queen, but return to my wealthy caftle, ' than be thus ufed.' The king commanded the prin- cefs immediately to alight, make it her requeft to Grog- non, that fhe would be pleafed to do her the honour to accept of her horfe.

The princefs obeyed without any reply; but Grognon took no notice of her, nor even thanked her for her civility; but caufing herfelf to be mounted, upon the princefs's fine ambler, fhe looked then if poffible, more odious and frightful than before; and all the while eight gentlemen held her for fear of falling. Neverthelefs fhe was not pleafed, but muttered a thoufand menaces and curfes between her gums. They afked her what fhe would be pleafed to have? ' Have! (faid fhe) why, as I am ' miftrefs here, I would have the green page to hold my ' horfe, as he did when Graciofa rode upon it.' Imme- diately the king ordered the green page to lead the queen's horfe. Upon which Percinet caft his eyes upon his miftrefs, and fhe her's upon him, without fpeaking fo much as one word: however, he obeyed; and all the court moved on, while the trumpets founded aloud; whereat Grognon was rejoiced, and thought to herfelf, fhe would not change her flat nofe and fkrew mouth for all Graciofa's beauty.

But when they leaft expected it, the mettled horfe began to caper and bounce, and at length fell a run- ning as if it had been for a race. Grognon held faft by the mane and the pommel of the faddle, and bawl'd out a moft hideous roar; but at length her courfer

threw

ᵗhrew her, and down she came with one foot in the stir-
rup, the horse dragging her over the stones, through
bushes, and through thick and thin, till she was all over
so bemired that it would have been a kindness to have
pumped her. But as the whole court rode after her as
fast as possible, they soon overtook her, though not till
her flesh was torn from her legs and thighs, her head
bruised in three or four places, and one arm broken;
in short, never was a royal bride in such a miserable
condition.

The king seemed to be at his wits end: they picked
her up like a glass broken in pieces; for her bonnet
lay in one place her shoes in another; there lay a row
of teeth, there lay an eye; they however carried her to
the king's palace, put her to bed, and sent for the most
eminent surgeons. But notwithstanding her disorder,
she continued to scold and rave without ceasing.

‘ This is one of Graciosa's tricks, (cried she) without
‘ doubt she picked out that unruly head-strong jade to
‘ do me a mischief, and to have killed me if she could.
‘ If the king does not do me justice, I'll return to my
‘ wealthy castle, and never see him more.’ Grognon's
wrathful speech was presently reported to the king; whose
prevailing passion being interest, the thoughts of losing
so many pipes of gold and diamonds made him tremble;
so that he was ready for any impression of revenge.
He ran to his odious mistress, fell at her feet, and swore,
that if she would think of a punishment proportionable
to Graciosa's offence, he would give her up to chastise-
ment: to which she answered, she was satisfied, and
would send for the wretch immediately.

Accordingly a messenger was sent to tell the princess
that Grognon would speak with her. The poor princess
immediately turned pale, and shook every joint of her,
believing that the message boded her no good, and that
it was not to caress and give her sweetmeats that Grognon
desired her company: she looked about her every where,
to see whether Percinet would, but there were no signs
of him; so she went with trembling feet and sad heart
to Grognon's apartment. No sooner was she entered,
but

but the doors were locked upon her, and four women, resembling four furies, fell upon her, tore her costly garments from her back, and stript off her very shift. But when they discovered her naked beauty, the cruel hags being unable to bear the lustre of her dazzling whiteness, shut their eyes, as if they had been gazing a long time upon the snow. ' Fall on, fall on, (cried the " merciless Grognon, from her bed) let me have her ' flayed, leave not a bit of that white skin, which she ' thinks so lovely, upon her flesh.

In any other distress Graciosa could have wished for her dear Percinet; but finding herself quite stript, she was too modest to desire the prince should be a witness to her nakedness, and therefore she prepared herself to suffer like a helpless lamb. The four furies had each of them a terrible rod in their hands, and huge brooms stood by them to make more, as they wore out the first: they laid on without mercy; and at every stroke Grognon cried out, harder, harder yet, you are too merciful.

Nobody would have thought, but that after all this, the princess must have been flayed alive from head to foot: but it fell out otherwise; for the courtly Percinet had bewitched the women's eyes, so that they thought they had rods in their hands, when they were only light plumes of various coloured feathers; which Graciosa immediately perceived, and ceased to be afraid. ' Oh, " Percinet, said she to herself, thou art come generously to my relief! What should I have done without ' thee?' The furies having at last so tired themselves, that they could no longer stir their arms, they huddled the princess's cloaths about her, and put her out of the room, with a great deal of injurious language.

The princess returned to her chamber, and feined to be very ill, went to bed, and ordered that nobody should stay in the room but her nurse, to whom she recounted the whole story, and, tired with telling it, fell asleep; which the nurse perceiving, went out of the chamber about business. Soon after, the princess waking, spied in a corner of the chamber, the green page, not daring to come any nearer out of respect. She told him she

would

would never forget the obligation he had laid upon her: she conjured him not to abandon her to the fury of her implacable enemy; and desired him for the present to retire, because she had often been told, that it was not decent for young virgins to be alone with young men. He replied, ' That he hoped she was sensible of the ' respect he had for her; and that it was but his duty, ' as she was his mistress, to obey her in all things, ' though it were at the expence of his own satisfaction.' He thereupon left her; having first advised her to feign herself ill from the severe treatment she had received.

Grognon's joy to hear that Graciosa was in such a weak condition, made her mend sooner than could have been expected: after which the nuptials were solemnized with a more than ordinary magnificence. And because the king knew that Grognon, above all things in the world, loved to be praised as a beauty, he caused her picture to be drawn, and proclaimed a tournament, wherein six of the bravest and most accomplished knights of the court were to maintain against all gainsayers, that Grognon was the most beautiful princess in the world. Many knights and strangers came to maintain the contrary. And the ugly queen was present at all the combats, placed in a balcony under a canopy of cloth of gold; where she had the pleasure to see her knights, by their strength and activity, victors, in defence of her bad cause. Graciosa, who was placed behind her, drew the eyes of all the people upon her, while the silly and vain-glorious Grognon thought herself the only object of their admiration.

At last, when none seemed to be left that durst defy the champions of Grognon's Beauty, on a sudden there arrived a young knight, holding in his hand a box that was all set with diamonds: immediately he caused proclamation to be made, that he would maintain Grognon to be the foulest and most deformed of all the sex, and that she, whose picture he had in his box, was the most beautiful virgin in the world. Having said this, he ran against all the six knights, and threw them to the ground. After which, six more presenting themselves, one after

another.

another till they numbered four and twenty, the young knight ferving them all alike; and then opening his box, he told the vanquifhed champions, that to convince them of their error, he fhould fhew them his beautiful picture. Every body immediately knew it to be the princefs Graciofa's, but who the young knight was, nobody could tell; who, after he had made a profound bow to his miftrefs, retired without telling his name: but Graciofa did not doubt he was her beloved Percinet.

The enraged Grognon, being almoft choaked with anger, and unable to fpeak, made figns that it was Graciofa fhe would be at; and when fhe could explain herfelf, fhe fell a raving like a bedlamite. ' How!' (faid ' fhe) difpute with the prize of beauty? What, bring ' her champion to affront my knights! No, it is not ' be borne.—I'll be revenged or die.' ' Madam, ' (replied the princefs) I will proteft to your majefty, I ' have no hand in this unlucky accident; and, if you ' pleafe will fign it with my blood, that you are the moft ' charming beauty in the world, and that I am a mon- ' fter of deformity.' ' Oh—you are merry, Mrs. Cock- ' a-hoop, (replied Grognon; but I fhall have my turn ' in a little time.' Prefently it was told the king in what a fury his wife was, and what a deadly fear the princefs was in; who befought him to have pity on her; for that if he left her to the queen's indignation, fhe would fhew her no mercy. But the king was not moved; and all his anfwer was, that as he had given up the princefs into the power of her mother-in-law, fhe might do what fhe pleafed with her.

The wicked Grognon waited with impatience for night; and when it was dark, ordered her flying-coach to be got ready; forced Graciofa into it, and directed her to be carried, under a good guard, a hundred leagues off, into a wide foreft, through which nobody durft travel, becaufe it was full of lions, bears, tygers, and wolves. When they were into the midft of this foreft, they ordered her to alight, and there left her, regardlefs of her tears and fupplications to take pity on her. ' I beg not (faid ' fhe) my life at your hands; but only that you will

. vouchfafe

‘ vouchfafe me a fpeedy death: kill me, and at once
‘ deliver me from the many terrors worfe than death
‘ that I am going to fuffer.’ But fhe might as well have
talked to fo many ftatues, for they would not even give
her an anfwer, and flying from her with an uncom-
paffionate fpeed, left the fair unfortunate virgin all alone.
Forfaken thus, and in the dark, fhe wandered for fome
time, not knowing whether fhe went, bruifing herfelf
fometimes againft the trees, falling fometimes, and
fometimes entangling among the thorns and bufhes; till
at length fhe fat down up n the ground, not having
ftrength to ftand on her feet. Percinet, fhe cried fometimes to herfelf. ‘ Oh Percinet! where art thou? Is it
‘ poffible that thou fhouldft forfake me?’ No fooner had
fhe uttered thefe words, but fhe faw one of the moft
agreeable and furpiifing fights in the world; it was an
illumination fo fplendid, that there was hardly a
tree in the foreft on which there did not hang feveral
branches ftuck with tapers; and at the bottom of a walk
fhe perceived a palace, which feemed to be all of chry-
ftal, and fhone as bright as the fun. She fecretly hoped
Percinet had a hand in this pleafing enchantment;
which hope infpired her with no fmall joy, though intermixed with fear. ‘ I am alone, (faid fhe to herfelf)
‘ the prince is young, agreeable, amorous, and I am
‘ obliged to him for my life: Oh - this is too, too much,
‘ I muft get out of his way; ’tis better I fhould die than
‘ yield to his love.’ Having uttered thefe words, fhe
arofe faint and weary as fhe was, as without fo much
as turning her eyes towards the fair caftle, walking
another way, fo difturbed by the diftraction of her
thoughts, that fhe knew not what fhe did.

At this inftant, a noife, which fhe heard behind her,
increafed her fears, and made her apprehend fome wild
beaft was coming to bevour her; but looking, trembling,
behind her, fhe perceived Percinet, who feemed more
beautiful than Love himfelf is painted by the moft ex-
‘ quifite pencils. What, (faid he) my adorable princefs,
‘ do you fly from me!—Are you afraid of him who adores
‘ you? Can it be, that you fhould have fo little know-

‘ ledge

'ledge of my refpect, as to believe me to be capable of
'failing in the duty I owe you? Ah, no, ceafe your fears,
'and go with me to the palace of Fairy-land; into which,
'however, I will deny myfelf the pleafure of entering, if
'you forbid me. There you will be received by the
'queen my mother, and my fifters, who already have a
'moft tender affection for you, from the report I have
'made of your rare endowments.' Graciofa, charmed
with the fubmiffive and obliging manner of her young
lover's addrefs, could not refufe to feat herfelf with him
in a little calafh, curioufly painted and gilded, which
two harts drew with fuch prodigious fwiftnefs, that in
a very fhort time he fhewed her a thoufand different
parts of the foreft, which filled her with admiration.
Every thing might be diftinctly feen. In one place,
fhepherds and fhepherdeffes, curioufly dreffed, and
dancing to their flutes and bagpipes. In other places,
by the fides of purling ftreams, fhe beheld the country
fwains courting their miftreffes, and heightening their
mirth by finging a thoufand witty fongs and roundelays,
'I thought (faid fhe to Percinet) this foreft had been
'uninhabited; but to me it feems to be well peopled,
'and that the people live very happily.'—'Since your
'coming hither, my dear princefs, (replied Percinet)
'this gloomy folitude has been the feat of delights and
'pleafing amufements: the loves and graces all wait
'on you; and the flowers, daifies and primrofes fpring
'up under your feet.' Graciofa durft make no reply,
being unwilling to engage in fuch kind of compliments,
and therefore defired the prince to carry her to the
queen his mother.

Immediately he commanded the harts to haften to
the palace of Fairy-land, whither when the princefs
came, her ears were entertained with the fweeteft
mufic; and the queen; with her two daughters, who
were all exquifitely beautiful, came forth to meet her,
embraced her, and led her into a great room, the walls
of which were of the fineft cryftal. There, with great
aftonifhment, fhe obferved the ftory of her life engraved
to that very day, ending with the tour fhe had juft taken

in

the foreſt with the prince in his calaſh. ' Your hiſtorians
' are very quick, (ſaid Gracioſa to Percinet) for I per-
' ceive all the variety of my actions, or even geſtures,
' are immediately recorded here.' ' The reaſon, my
' dear princeſs, (replied Percinet) is, becauſe I would
' not loſe the moſt minute idea of your perfections, but
' imprint them deeply in my heart; yet, alas! I am
' neither happy nor contented any where.' She anſwered him not a word, but thanked the queen for her
kind reception. Soon after a noble banquet was ſerved
up, and Gracioſa eat with good appetite; being overjoyed to meet with Percinet in the foreſt, where ſhe had
been afraid ſhe ſhould have found nothing but bears and
lions. And now, though ſhe was ſufficiently tired, he
engaged her to go into a large room that glittered with
gold and diamonds, and contained the moſt exquiſite
paintings, where ſhe was entertained with an opera, de-
ſcribing the loves of Cupid and Pſyche, intermixt with
dances and ſongs, among which a young ſhepherd ſung
the following:

> You are belov'd fair Gracioſa, more
> Than ere the God of Love himſelf could love,
> When he is Pſyche did adore.
> Be not more rig'rous than bears or wolves,
> Whoſe natural rage diſſolves,
> When liking and affection move.
> They to love's laws ſubmit and tamely pay
> Their homage to the little archer's bow.
> Why ſhould not you
> As tender be, and kinder far than they?

She bluſh'd to hear herſelf thus named before the
queen and the princeſſes; and whiſpered Percinet, that
ſhe was aſhamed to find all the world were privy to their
ſecrets; which, continued ſhe, puts me in mind of ſome
pretty lines, which may be aptly applied on this occaſion.

> Keep your ſecrets in your breaſt:
> Silence is a charming gueſt,
>   I entertain with full content:
>   For the worlds as ſtrange conceits,
>   And, as crimes, too often treats
>   The pleaſures of the innocent.

Percinet

Percinet begged her pardon for having done a thing that difpleafed her   And now, the opera being at an end, the queen ordered the two princeffes to conduct Graciofa to her apartment.   Nothing was ever more magnificent than the chamber and furniture, nor forich as the bed where fhe was to lie.   She was attended by four and twenty virgins dreffed like nymphs, the eldeft of which was about eighteen, and every one feemed to be a miracle of beauty.   When fhe was in bed, a moft heavenly fymphony of mufic filled the room, to lull her to fleep; but her fpirits were fo agitated and difordered by thefe furprifing things, that it was not in her power to clofe her eyes.   ‘ All that I have feen (faid fhe) ‘ muft certainly be Enchantments.   Good heavens! ‘ that a prince fo agreeable and witty fhould be fo ‘ formidable!   I cannot make too much hafte from thefe ‘ enchanting places.’   Yet when fhe confidered the agreeable difference bet een living in fo magnificent a palace, and expofing herfelf to the cruelty of the barbarous Grognon, fhe could not think of the feparation without regret.   This confideration pleaded for her ftay; but, on the other fide, fhe found Percinet fo obliging, that fhe refolved not to continue any longer in a palace, of which ne was the mafter.

In the morning, as foon as fhe was up, fhe was prefented with garments of all forts and colours, and the richeft jewels, laces, gloves, and filk ftockings; all extremely fine, and admirable for the curiofity of their workmanfhip.   Graciofa's drefs was never before fo fplendid, nor did fhe ever more gracefully become it, nor appear fo charming.   When fhe was dreffed, Percinet entered her chamber, habited in green and gold, for green was his colour, becaufe Graciofa loved it. Whatever is admirable in fhape, beauty of features, and majeflicnefs of mien, was all exquifitely perfect in Percinet.   Graciofa told him fhe had not flept a wink all night; having been kept awake by the thoughts of her misfortunes; and that fhe could not but be apprehenfive of the confequences.   ‘ What are your fears, ‘ madam? (replied Percinet) You are abfolute fovereign

' 'reign here, and are adored; will you then forfake
' 'me and return to your moſt cruel enemy?' ' Were I
' the miſtreſs of my own deſtiny, (anſwered the princeſs)
' I would willingly accept the choice you propoſe; but
' I am accountable for my actions to the king my father;
' and it is better, therefore, for me to ſuffer, than be
' wanting in my duty.' Percinet omitting nothing that
he could think of to perſuade her to marry him; but ſhe
would by no means give her conſent; and it was almoſt
againſt her will that he detained her eight days; during
which time he entertained her with a thouſand new plea-
ſures and diverſions.

While ſhe ſtayed, ſhe ſeveral times expreſſed an
earneſt deſire to know what paſſed in Grognon's court;
and what plauſible ſtories ſhe contrived to conceal the
cruelty of her intentions. Percinet told her he would
ſend his 'ſquire, who was both witty and diſcreet. The
princeſs replied, ' She was perſuaded he needed nobody
' to inform him, but might tell her himſelf.' ' Come
' then (ſaid he) with me to the great tower, and you
' ſhall there directly ſee with your own eyes what you
deſire to know.' With that he led her to a tower that
was prodigiouſly high, and all of cryſtal of the rock, like
the reſt of the caſtle. He bid her ſet her foot in a particular place, and put her little finger in his mouth, and
then look towards the city. Which ſhe had no ſooner
done, but ſhe perceived the wicked Grognon ſitting with
the king, and heard her talking with him after this manner: ' This poor wretch, the princeſs, with all her beau-
' ty, has hanged herſelf in the cellar: I have been to ſee
' her, and I profeſs the very ſight of her frighted me:
' All that is now to be done is to bury her, and then I
' make no queſtion but your majeſty will ſoon forget ſo
' inconſiderable a loſs.' But the king wept, and bewailed
the death of his daughter, while Grognon deriding his
ſorrows, retired to her chamber; where, by her command, a large billet was preſently dreſſed up in fune-
ral pomp, and laid in a coffin, and the king immediately ordered a ſolemn interment. Infinite was the
train of mourners that attended the hearſe, weeping and
                                                    wailing

wailing, and bitterly curfing the ftep-dame, whom they fecretly accufed as the caufe of the princefs's death. Every body went into deep mourning; and the princefs could hear them lamenting to themfelves, What pity it was, fo fweet and young a princefs fhould perifh through the cruelty of the wicked Grognon! It were a good deed, they cried, to cut her to pieces, and caft her to the fowls of the air. The king alfo would neither eat nor drink, but grieved continually.

Graciofa feeing her father fo extremely afflicted, ' Ah, Percinet (faid fhe) 'tis impoffible for me longer ' to bear that my father fhould think me dead; there- ' fore, if you love me, carry me back again, that I may ' fhew myfelf at court.' Notwithftanding all his argu- ments, he could not prevail upon her to relinguifh this requeft. ' Dear princefs (faid he) you will wifh your- ' felf again, more than once in the palace of Fairy-land; ' though I dare not prefume you will ever wifh for me, ' to whom you are more cruel even than Grognon is ' to you.' But whatever he could fay, Graciofa infifted upon going: fo taking leave of the princefs, mother and fifters, Percinet and fhe got into the calafh, and the harts ran with the fwiftnefs of arrows. When they were out of the precincts of the palace, Graciofa heard a great noife; and looking behind her, beheld the whole edifice tumbled down, and fhattered into a thoufand pieces. ' What miracle is this, (faid fhe) the palace quite ' demolifhed!—Yes, madam, (replied Percinet) I muft ' have my palace among the dead, nor will you ever ' enter it again till your death.' ' Why are you angry? ' (replied Graciofa, endeavouring to pacify him) all ' things confidered, have I not more reafon to com- ' plain than you?'

When they arrived at the court, Percinet fo ordered it, that himfelf, the princefs, and the calafh, became invifible; fo that fhe went unfeen till fhe come into the king's chamber, and threw herfelf at his feet. When the king faw her, he ftarted up in fear, and was running away, taking her for a ghoft; but fhe held him by his garment, and convinced him fhe was not dead; but that Grognon

Grognon had caufed her to be carried into a wild foreft,
where fhe had got into a tree, and lived upon the fruit.
She added, that the queen had caufed a billet to be
buried inftead of her; and befought him to fend her to
one of his remote caftles, where fhe might not be expofed
to the rage of her mother-in-law.

The king, doubted whether fhe fpoke truth, fent to
have the billet taken up, and being convinced of the
impofture, was amazed at Grognon's wickednefs, not
imagining fuch malice could have been in a woman's
breaft. Any other king would have laid her in the billet's place: but he was a poor weak man, who had no
courage to be angry in carneft: however, he careffed
his daughter more than ever, and made her fup with
him. But when Grognon's creatures acquainted her
with the princefs's return, and that fhe had fupped with
the king, her rage became perfect frenzy. She flew to
the king's chamber, and told him, he muft either deliver
up his daughter to her that moment, or fhe would inftantly be gone and never fee him more; that he was a
fool to believe fhe was Graciofa, though indeed fhe fomewhat refembled her, for that Graciofa had certainly
hanged herfelf; and that if he gave credit to the impofture of others, he had not the confidence and value
which he ought to have for her The king, not daring
to refift, delivered up the unfortunate princefs into her
hands, believing, or feigning to believe, fhe was not his
daughter.

Grognon, tranfported with joy, dragged the princefs,
by the help of her women, into a dark dungeon, where
fhe caufed her to be ftripped, covered her with courfe
dirty rags, and a nafty cap upon her head, hardly allowed
her ftraw to lie upon, or bread to eat.

In this diftrefs fhe wept bitterly, and wifhed herfelf
again in the caftle of Fairy-land; but fhe durft not call
upon Percinet, confcious that fhe had not been fo kind
to him as fhe ought to have been; and confequently not
daring to promife herfelf, that he had ftill fo much love
for her, as to come again to her fuccour. In the mean
time the wicked Grognon had fent for a Fairy more
malicious

malicious than herfelf; who being come, ' I have got
' (faid fhe) a little faucy minx that vexes me to death?
' I would willingly punifh her, by fetting her fome diffi-
' cult talks, which the not being able to accomplifh, I
' may have a pretence to break her bones and the no
' excufe: affift me, therefore, to find out fome new
' punifhment tor her every day.' The Fairy anfwered,
fhe would conlider of it, and return the next day. She
was as good as her word, and brought with her a fkain
of thread, as wide about as the waift of three people;
fo fine that it wou'd hardly bear breathing upon; and
fo tangled, that neither beginning or end were to be
found. Grognon was overjoyed at the impoffibility of
this talk; fent immediately for the lovely captive, and,
with a fmile of derifion, ' Here, (faid fhe) prepare
' your clumfey paws to unravel this fkain; and be
' affured, if thou breakeft the leaft bit, thou fhalt dearly
' pay for it; for I will flay thee alive myfelf: begin
' when thou wilt, but I muft have it unravelled before
' fun-fet;' and, laying this, fhe fhut her up in a chamber
under three locks.

When the princefs was alone, fhe attempted the talk,
turning the fkain a thoufand ways, and broke it a thoufand times; which fo diftracted her that fhe gave over
the attempt; and throwing it in the middle of the room,
' Go, fatal fkain, (faid fhe) lie there, fince thou it is
' that art to be the occafion of my death. Oh, Percinet!
' Percinet! if my feverity has not given too great a
' repulfe to your affection, though I cannot hope your
' affiftance, yet come, however, and receive my laft
' farewell.' Saying this, fhe fell a weeping fo bitterly,
that any thing lefs fenfible than a lover would have been
moved to compaffion. Percinet immediately opened
the door with the fame eafe as if he had the kevs in his
pocket. ' Here I am, dear princefs, (faid he) always
' ready at your fervice; it is not in my power to for-
' fake you, though you refufe to return my love.'
Having faid this, he ftruck three times with his wand
upon the fkain; and immediately the threads untwifted,
and clofed one to the other; and with two more ftrokes,
the

the whole was unravelled with furprifing eafe: which
done, he afked her, whether fhe had any other fervice to
command him, and whether fhe intended never to bear
his company, but in her diftreffes? ' Upbraid me not,
' fweet Percinet (cried fhe) I am already too unfor-
' tunate.——Oh, princefs, (replied Percinet) it is your
' own fault that you are not abfolutely delivered from
' this infulting tyranny, to which you are a victim.
' Go with me, make your felicity mine, and mine yours;
' what are you afraid of! That you love me not with
' a fincere and lafting affection: (replied the princefs)
' I am defirous that time fhould confirm the truth of
' the fentiments you exprefs for me.' Percinet being
offended at her jealoufy, took his leave and left her.

The fun was juft fetting, when Grognon, who waited
for the clofe of the evening with the greateft impatience,
came with her four furies, who attended her wherever
fhe went. She put her three keys into the three locks,
and as fhe opened the door, ' Well! (faid fhe) I fup-
' pofe my beautiful idler has been afraid to make ufe
' of her ten fingers.—Ay, ay, fhe had rather fleep to
preferve her complexion.' However, when fhe was entered, Graciofa prefented to her the fkain, wherein there
was not a thread amifs; fo that all Grognon could fay
was, that fhe had fullied it, and was an awkward creature! for which fhe gave her two fuch unmerciful blows
on her fair cheeks, which were of the colour of the lily
and the rofe, that they became black and blue. The
unfortunate Graciofa, who was forced to fuffer patiently
what fhe could not avoid, was after this locked clofe up
again in her dungeon.

Grognon amazed that fhe had fucceeded no better
with her fkain of thread, fent for the Fairy again; and
reproached her in very paffionate terms; ' Find me
' out fomething elfe, (faid fhe) fo difficult as may
' amount to an impoffibility.' The Fairy went away,
and the next day returned with a great tub full of feathers of all forts of birds; as nightingales, canary birds,
robin-redbreafts, goldfinches, linnets, parrots, owls,
fparrows, pigeons, oftriches, buftards, peacocks, larks,

partridges, and an infinite number more, which I am unable to name; and thefe feathers were fo intermixed, that the birds themfelves would never have been able to have known their own apparel. ' Here (faid the ' fairy to Grognon) is that will try the wit and pa- ' tience of your captive: command her to feparate ' thefe feathers, and lay the plumage of every one of ' thefe birds by itfelf! which is a tafk would puzzle her, ' where fhe a Fairy herfelf.' Grognon was in an ecftafy of joy only at the bare thoughts of the princefs's per- plexity. She fent for her; and after having terrified her with a thoufand menaces, fhe fhut her up with the feathers in a chamber under three locks, as before; giv- ing her to underftand, that fhe expected her work fhould be done before fun-fet.

Graciofa took fome of the feathers, and looked upon them; but finding it impoffible to know the difference of one bird's feathers from thofe of another, fhe threw them back into the tub. Yet fhe made feveral effays: but the oftener fhe try'd, the more impoffible fhe found her tafk. So that, at length overwhelmed with grief and defpair, ' I muft die, (faid fhe, with a lamentable voice) ' it is my death that is fought for, and only that can ' put an end to my miferies. Injured Percinet, has ' left me too no doubt; and to call upon him for fuccour, ' would be in vain; for, had his love continued, he ' would have been here ere now.'

' Dear Graciofa, I am here, cried Percinet, ftarting ' up from under the feathers, where he lay hid) I am ' ready to deliver you from all your troubles: and now, ' after fo many proofs of my fidelity, can you any ' longer fufpect the fincerity of my affection, or think I ' do not love you better than my life?'. Saying this, he ftruck three times with his wand upon the cafk, and immediately the feathers flew out, and forted them- felves into little heaps about the room. ' I am in- ' finitely obliged to you, Sir, (faid Graciofa) but for ' you, I muft have been loft: and be affured I will not ' be ungrateful.' The prince ufed his utmoft endea- vours to perfuade her to come to an immediate refolu- tion

tion in his favour: but still she insisted upon time, he complied, though it was much against his will.

Grognon came exactly at her hour; but was quite amazed and confounded to see her designs again defeated: she, however, bestowed some blows upon Graciosa, pretending the feathers were not laid even. She sent for the Fairy directly, and fell into such a rage against her, that she knew not what to say, being herself quite confounded. At length the Fairy promised to use her utmost art, in making a box, which if her curiosity ever tempted her to open, should puzzle her to shut again, beyond all the arts in Fairy land to help her: Accordingly some days after, she brought this box, which was somewhat large. ' Here, (said she to Grog-
' non) send your captive somewhere with this box;
' but forbid her to open it, and then she certainly will;
' and you will have your desire.' Grognon, observing the Fairy's directions, ' Here, (said she, to her fair
' captive) carry this box to my rich castle, and set it
' upon a table in my cabinet; but, upon pain of death,
' I command you not to look what is in it.'

Graciosa, having put on her wooden clogs, her canvas gown, and her woollen cap, set out on her journey. All that met her cried, certainly there goes some goddess in disguise; for the poverty of her dress could not conceal her wonderful beauty. However, she began to be tired with her journey; and coming into a little wood, surrounded with delightful meadows, she sat down to rest herself: but having set the box on her knees, her curiosity on a sudden prompted her to open it. ' What can
' be the danger; said she to herself) I shall take no-
' thing out of it, and would only see what is in it;' so, reflecting no farther on the consequences, she opened the box; when immediately out came a great many little men and women, violins, instruments, little pictures, little cooks, and little dishes; in short, the giant of the whole company was not higher than your little finger: they danced in the meadows; divided themselves into companies, and began the pleasantest ball that ever was seen; some skipped and capered about; others acted as

cooks;

cooks; some eat and drank; and the little violins played
to a miracle. Graciofa, for fome time, was delighted
with the fight, thinking to recall the merry wantons
into the box; but not one of them would return: the
little gentlemen and ladies betook themfelves to their
heels; the violins ran away; the cooks, with their pots
upon their heads, and their fpits upon their fhoulders,
flew from her like fo many birds; and when fhe followed
them into the wood, they got into the meadows; when
fhe ran after them in the meadows, they flew into the
wood. ' Oh, indiferret curiofity! (cried Graciofa,
' weeping) Now my enemies will prevail: the only
' misfortune I could have prevented, is befallen me
' through my own folly; no, I cannot fufficiently
' blame myfelf. Oh! Percinet! Percinet! if it be
' poffible for thee ftill to love a princefs fo imprudent,
' affift me once more, in this moft perilous accident
' that ever threatened my life.

Percinet did not ftay to be called thrice, but appeared
immediately in his green habit; faying, were it not for
the wicked Grognon, he fuppofed Graciofa would never
think of him. ' Have a better opinion of my fenti-
' ments (replied the princefs) I am neither infenfible
' of merit, nor ungrateful for kindneffes received. It
' is true, I have put your conftancy to trials; but it
' is to crown it when I am convinced of it.' Percinet
being now better pleafed than ever, gave three ftrokes
with his wand upon the box, and immediately the little
gentlemen and ladies, the violins, the cooks, with their
roaft meat, in fhort, the whole of this deminutive company placed themfelves again in the box, as if they had
never been out of it. Which done, Percinet, who had
left his chariot in the wood, defired the princefs to ufe
it the remaining part of her journey to the caftle; and
indeed fhe had no fmall need of fuch a convenience,
confidering the condition fhe was in. So, having rendered her invifible, he conducted her himfelf, and by
that means had the pleafure of her company; a pleafure to which, my chronicle fays, fhe was not indifferent
in her heart, though fhe was careful to conceal her fen-
ments.

D   Thus

Thus she arrived at the rich castle: but when she demanded the key of the cabinet in Grognon's name, the governor burst out a laughing. —' How! (said he) hast ' thou the confidence to think that shepherds girls are ' ever admitted into queens cabinets! Go, go, get thee ' gone, wooden clogs and hobnails never yet defiled ' these glittering floors.' Graciosa desired him to write a line why he had refused her entrance, which he readily did. So leaving the castle, she was received by the amiable Percinet, who waited for her, and conducted her back to the king's palace. It would be difficult to relate all the tender and respectful arguments he used by the way, to persuade her to put an end to her misfortunes. To which she replied, that if Grognon imposed upon her any more of these impossible commands, she would yield him her consent.

When the enraged step-dame saw the princess returned, she flew upon the fairy, whom she had detained with her all the while, fastened her claws in her wrinkled cheeks, and would have throttled her too, had it been possible to strangle a Fairy. Graciosa presented her the governor's letter and the box; but she threw both in the fire, not vouchsafing to open them; and had she thought of it, would have thrown the princess after them; but she did not defer her punishment.

She caused a great hole to be made in the garden, as deep as a well, and a great stone to be laid over the mouth of it. Then taking occasion to walk in the garden, she said to Graciosa, and the rest that attended her, ' Under that stone, as I am informed, there lies concealed immense treasure, let us go and remove it.' Upon this, they all set their hands to it, and Graciosa among the rest; which was what Grognon desired; for as the princess stood by the side of the hole, Grognon pushed her in, and then rolled the stone over it again.

This stroke appeared past remedy; for how could Percinet find her thus buried in the earth? She herself despaired, and repented she had so long delayed to marry him. ' How terrible is my destiny: (said she) this ' kind of death is more dreadful than any other.

Oh,

' Oh, Percinet! you are fufficiently revenged for my
' fcrupulous reluctancy. But I was afraid you were
' like many other men, who prove inconftant when
' once they find themfelves beloved; I was defirous to
' be certain of your heart, but my unjuft fufpicions are
' now the caufe of my prefent mifery. Yet, (con-
' tinued fhe) if I could but hope you would fhew fome
' regret for the lofs of me, I fhould be lefs fenfible of
' my misfortune.' She was lamenting in this manner
to eafe her forrows, when fhe perceived a little door
open, which fhe had not feen before, by reafon of the
obfcurity. At the fame time fhe alfo faw day-light, and
a garden full of flowers, fruits, fountains, grottos,
ftatutes, groves, and arbours; fhe went in, and walked
forward into a fpacious alley, wondering what would be
the event of this extraordinary beginning. Soon after
fhe difcovered the caftle of Fairy-Land, which fhe
eafily knew again; for a caftle made all of cryftal of
the rock, with the hiftory of one's life engraved therein,
is no very common fight. Percinet appeared too, together with the queen his mother, and his fifters.
' Fair princefs (faid the queen to Graciofa) it is time
' now you fhould confent; make my fon moft happy,
' and free yourfelf from that deplorable condition
' wherein you live under the tyranny of Grognon.

The grateful princefs fell upon her knees, and told
the queen fhe might difpofe of her deftiny, and that fhe
would obey her in all things; that now fhe difcovered
the truth of Percinet's prediction, when he foretold her,
that his palace fhould be among the dead, and fhe never
enter it again, till fhe had been buried; that fhe was
amazed at his knowledge, that his merit was no lefs her
admiration, and therefore fhe accepted him for her
hufband. Now the prince, in his turn, threw himfelf
at her feet; the whole palace refounded with mufic and
acclamations of joy; and the nuptials were folemnized
with the greateft magnificence. All the fairies for a
thoufand miles round came thither in moft fumptuous
equipages; fome in chariots drawn by fwans, others by
dragons; fome rode upon the clouds, and others in

globes

globes of fire. Among the latter appeared the Fairy who affifted Grognon to torment Graciofa. When fhe knew who it was, fhe was in the greateft furprife; befought her to forget what was paft, and faid fhe would endeavour to make her amends for the evils fhe had caufed her to fuffer. And it is certain, fhe did not ftay out the feftival, but remounted her chariot drawn by two terrible ferpents, fhe flew to the king's palace; and finding Grognon out, wrung off her neck, notwithftanding what all the guards and her women could do to prevent it.

The MORAL.

Detefted envy thus with baneful wing,
    Difturbs the calm of our fereneft days;
She ne'er with-holds her poifon'd fting,
    But wounds infidious, and our peace betrays.

'Twas fhe who Grognon's malice mov'd
    To ruin Graciofa's innocence;
'Twas fhe who all thefe fnares improv'd
    Her wit to baffle, and confound her fenfe.

'Twas fhe who aim'd the cruel darts,
    Fair Graciofa's peace undoing;
But Percinet their influence thwarts,
    And faves the fair from ruin.

Well did he then deferve the heart,
    Which afterwards fhe gave his love;
And who with firmnefs bear the fmart,
    To perfect joy their pains improve.

THE

CURIOUS STORY.

OF

FINETTA.

SOME time ago there lived a king and queen who had managed their affairs fo ill, that they were driven out of their dominions; and to fupport themfelves, were forced to fell their crowns, then their robes, linen, and laces, and afterwards all they had; and when they were reduced to the utmoſt poverty, the king faid to the queen, ' We are forced out of our kingdoms, ' and have nothing left, therefore we muſt think of ' getting a livelihood both for ourfelves and children; ' think a little what we fhould do; for my part I am ' entirely at a lofs.' The queen who was a woman of good fenfe and wit, aſked eight days time to confider of it; and when they were expired, faid to him, ' Come, ' don't let us vex and torment ourfelves; you fhall ' lay nets and fnares for fowls and lines for fifh, while ' I make them: As for our daughters, they are three ' proud idle fluts, and fancy themfelves ſtill to be great ' ladies, we will carry them a great way off, that it will ' be impoſſible for them to find their way back again; ' for we can never keep them as fine as they expect ' we fhould.'

The king, who was a kind father, began to weep when he faw he muſt part with his children; but the queen being of an imperious haughty temper, and he being forced to acquiefce with her, he told her fhe might rife

early

early the next morning and carry her daughters were she thought fit. While they were thus contriving this affair, the princefs Finetta, who was the youngeft of the three, heard them through the key-hole; and as foon as fhe was informed of their defign, ran as faft as fhe was able to a large grotto, inhabited by the Fairy Merlucha, her god-mother; but before fhe went, took two pounds of frefh butter, eggs, milk and flower, to make a cake of, that fhe might be the more acceptable gueft. When fhe firft fet out, fhe went very cheerfully; but after fhe had walked fome time, and the foles of her fhoes were worn away, and her feet began to be galled with the pebbles, fhe was fo weary, that fhe fat herfelf down on the grafs, and fell a-crying when a fine Spanifh horfe paffed by ready bridled and faddled, with diamonds enough on his houfings to buy two or three towns; who when he faw the princefs, he fed by her, bending his knees, feeming to pay fome refpect to her; whereupon taking him by the bridle, fhe faid, ' Pretty horfe, if you would carry me to my ' god-mother the Fairy, I fhall be very much obliged to ' thee; for I am fo weary, that I am ready to die ' away; I promife you I'll give you good corn and hay, ' and litter you down with clean ftraw.' The horfe bent down before her, and fhe jumped upon his back, he carried her to the Fairy's grotto as fwift as a bird flies in the air; for Merlucha knowing of her god-daughter's coming, had fent him for that purpofe.

When fhe went in, fhe made three low courtefies, kif-fed the hem of her garment, and then faid to her, ' Good ' morrow god-mother, how do you do? I have brought ' you here fome milk, butter, flower and eggs, to make ' a cake after our country fafhion.' ' You are welcome, ' Finetta, (faid the fairy) come and let me embrace ' you.' Whereupon fhe kiffed her two or three times, which made Finetta ready to die with joy; for Merlucha was a great and renowned fairy. ' Well my girl, ' (faid fhe) you fhall be my waiting woman, come ' drefs and comb my head; (which the princefs did ' with all the addrefs imaginable.) I know what brought ' you hither, (faid Merlucha) you heard the king and
queen

' queen confulting how they might lofe you, and you
' have no mind to be fo ferved. Take this clue of
' thread, it will not break, and faften one end of it to
' the door of your houfe, and keep the other in your
' hand ; when the queen leaves you, it will be an eafy
' matter for you, by this thread, to find your way back
' again.'

The princefs thanked her god mother, who gave her
a fack full of cloaths, all covered over with gold and filver, and embracing her, fet her upon the fame horfe
again, who carried her home in a moment or two ; and
when fhe had thanked her pretty horfe for his trouble,
and had bid him return, fhe went foftly into the houfe,
and hiding her fack under the bed, laid herfelf down
without taking any notice of what had paffed. As foon
as it was day, the king awakened his wife, and bid her
prepare for her journey : upon which fhe got up, and
put on a ftrong pair of fhoes, a fhort petticoat, and
white waiftcoat, and taking her ftick in her hand, went
to call her daughters ; the eldeft of whom was named
Love's Flower, the fecond Fair-Night, and the youngeft
Auricular, or Fine-Ear, but, by way of nick name Finetta.
' I have dreamed to-night, (faid the queen) that we
' muft go and fee my fifter, where we fhall be treated,
' and be very merry.' ' Well good madam, where you
' pleafe (faid Love's Flower) who could not endure to
' live in a defert, fo that we go but, 'tis no matter where.'
The other two faid the fame, and taking their leave of
their father, they all four fet forward for their journey
They went at laft fo far that Fine-Ear began to fear left
her clue fhould not hold out ; for they had gone a great
many fcore miles : however, fhe was always behind,
faftening her thread in the briars. When the queen
thought fhe had carried them fo far that they could not
find the way back again, fhe went into a large wood, and
faid to them, ' Come my little lambs, lie down and
' take a nap, while I, like a fhepherdefs, will watch you,
' left the wolf fhould furprife you.' Whereupon they
laid themfelves down and fell afleep, and the queen,
when fhe thought them faft, took her leave as fhe thought,

for

for the laft time, when Finetta, who only fhut her eyes, and pretended fleep, faid to herfelf, ' Was I now of a ' revengeful temper, I fhould leave my fifters to perifh ' here; for they have beat and abufed me very much; ' but, however, I will not forfake them.'—Whereupon waking them, fhe told them the whole ftory; at which they fell a-crying, and begged of her to take them along with her, promifing to give her all the fine things they had. ' I know, (faid Finetta) you will not perform ' what you promife; but neverthelefs I fhall act the ' part of a kind fifter.' And thereupon fhe rofe up, and followed the thread, which brought them home almoft -as foon as the queen.

When they came there, ftopping a moment at the door, they beard the king fay, ' My heart aches to fee ' you alone.' ' Indeed (faid the queen) we were very '' much troubled with our daughters ' ' Well, (faid ' the king) had you brought my Finetta back, I fhould ' not be fo much concerned for the other two.' And juft then they knocked at the door: ' Who's there?' ' (faid the king) ' Your three daughters, Love's Flower, ' Fair Night, and Fine-Ear, (replied they.') And at that the queen trembled, and faid, ' Don't open the ' door, for they are certainly their fpirits; for 'tis im- ' poffible they fhould be returned.' The king, who was as great a coward as his wife, faid, ' 'Tis falfe, you are ' not my daughters.' Whereupon Finetta replied, ' Look through the key-hole, papa, and if I am not your ' daughter, Finetta, I confent to be whipped.' At that the king did as fhe bid him, and knowing them opened the door. The queen feemed to be very glad to fee them, pretending fhe came back for fomething fhe had forgot, and defigned to have gone back to them again.

Finetta, when all was over, afked her fifters for what they had promifed her; who, thereupon beat her with their diftaffs, and told her, That it was for her fake that the king was not forry for them. Afterwards fhe went to bed; but being not able to fleep for the blows and bruifes they had given her, fhe heard the queen fay, fhe would carry them another way farther off, from whence

fhe

she was affured they would never return. Upon this
she got up foftly, went into the hen-houfe, and wrung
off the necks of two pullets and a cockerel, which the
queen had fet up to regale herfelf with; and putting
them into a bafket, fet out to go and fee her god-mother
again. She had not gone half a mile, being in the
dark, and frightened out of her wits, before she heard
the Spanifh horfe whinnying and prancing; who no
fooner came to her, but she mounted, and was carried
prefently to her god-mother's. After the ufual compliments, she prefented her with the fowls, and defired her
good advice; for that the queen had fworn to carry
them to the world's end. Merlucha bid her not grieve
herfelf, and gave her a fack full of afhes to carry before
her, to fprinkle before her as she went along, telling her
when she returned, she needed but obferve her foot-fteps,
which would conduct her back again; and withal, charged
her not to take her fifters along with her, affuring her,
if she did, she never would fee her more. The horfe
being ready, Finetta took her leave, and with it a great
quantity of diamonds in a box, which she put in her
pocket. A little before day, the queen called the princeffes again, and told them that the king was not very
well, and that she dreamed they muft go all four to
gather fome herbs for him in a certain country, were
they were excellent. Love's Flower and Fair-Night, who
fufpected that their mother's main end in this affair was
to lofe them, were very much afflicted; but were, notwithftanding, obliged to go, Finetta faid not a word all
the time, but kept behind them ftrewing her afhes! and
the queen being perfuaded that they would never be
able to find the way back, for she had carried them a
great diftance off, and obferving them all afleep one
evening, took that opportunity to bid them good-bye.
When it was day, that Finetta perceived her mother
was gone, she awakened her fifters, and told them the
queen was gone again, and had left them to themfelves.
Love's Flower and Fair-Night cried, and tore their hair,
and beat their breafts; when Finetta, who was a good-
natured girl, pitied them, and told them, though her

D 5   god-mother,

god-mother, when she informed her how she should find
the way back, charged her not to take them along with
her, and said she would never see her more if she did.
' Yet, (said she) I will venture this to preserve my
' sisters.' Whereupon they both fell upon her neck,
and kissed her, and all three returned together.

The king and queen were very much surprised to see
the princesses again, and talked about it all the night;
when Fine-Ear, who had not her name for nothing,
heard them lay a new plot, which the queen was to put
in execution in the morning, and thereupon ran and
awakened her sisters, and acquainted them with it.
' Alas! (said she) we are all lost, the queen without dif-
' pute will carry us and leave us in some desert; for
' your sakes I have disobliged my god-mother, and dare
' not go to her as I used to do.' This news put them to
their wits end, and made them say to one another, What
shall we do? ' Oh! (said Fair-Night) do not let us
' trouble ourselves, there are others who have as much
' contrivance as the old Melucha; we need but take
' some pease along with us, and sow them, and we shall
' easily trace our way back again.' Upon Love's-Flower approving this expedient, they put pease in their
pockets; but for Fine-Ear, instead of pease, she took her
sack of fine cloths, and her box of jewels; and they were
all three ready against the queen called. ' I have
' dreamed to-night (said she) that there are three prin-
' ces in a country I need not name, waiting to marry
' you, and I have a great mind to carry you to see whe-
' ther my dream is true or not.' The queen went first,
and the princesses followed after, sowing their pease as
they went along, never disturbing themselves, but being
satisfied that they, by that means, would find their way
home; when one dark night the queen left them again,
and went home to the king both weary of so long a journey, and glad to have got rid of so great a charge.

The three princesses slept till eleven o'clock the next day,
when Finetta discovered first the queen's absence; and
though she was well provided, could not forbear crying;
but, however, relied more on the Fairy Melucha, than
she

the ability of her fifters. ' The queen is gone (faid
' fhe to her fifters) let us follow her as faft as we can.'
' H ll your tongue, you fool (replied Love's-Flower)
' we can find the way when we pleafe.' Finetta durft return no anfwer; but when they wanted to go home,
they could find no traces or appearance of any peafe;
for the pigeons, with which that country abounded, had
eaten them up, which fet them all in tears. After
they had been two days without eating, Love's-Flower
afked her fifters, if they had nothing to eat? Whereupon
Finetta faid, fhe had found an acorn; which they would
have had from her; but fhe anfwered, ' What
' fignifies one acorn among three of us? Let us fet it,
' it may grow to a large tree, and be ferviceable.' To
which they all confented, though there was no likelihood
of any tree in that country, where there was nothing to
be feen but cabbages and lettuces, which the princeffes
lived on; for had they been nice, they muft have pe-
rifhed. They had no other covering, when they flept,
than the azure fkies, and watering their acorn every
night and morning, which they perfieved grew apace.
When it was got to fome fize, Love's-Flower was for
climbing it, but it was too weak to bear her; as was
likewife Fair-Night, but fhe was too heavy: whereupon
Finetta tried, and when fhe was up, her fifters afked her
what fhe faw? fhe told them nothing. ' Alas! (faid
' Love's-Flower,) this oak is not yet tall enough.' However, they kept watering of it, and Finetta never failed
to get up into it twice a-day, and one day when fhe was
up, Fair-Night faid to Love's-Flour, ' I have found
' a fack which our fifter has hid from us, what can there
' be in it?' ' Oh, (faid Love's Flower) fhe told me fhe
' had fome old laces.' ' But I believe fhe had fome-
' thing better,' replied Fair-Night. And being curious,
opened it, and found fome old laces of the king and
queen's, which ferved only to cover the fine clothes and
jewels. ' What a fly flut this is, faid fhe, let us take
' them away, and put fome pebbles in their place.'
Which the other agreeing to, Finetta came down again,
without ever difcovering the trick her fifters had played
her;

her: for she had no occasion to dress in a desert, all her thoughts being employed on her oak.

One morning when she was up in it, and her sisters asked her as usual, what she discovered, she told them she saw a house so beautiful, that she could not describe it, that the walls were of emeralds and rubies, and the roof of diamonds set in gold. ‘ You tell fibs, (said they) ‘ it cannot be so.’ ‘ Indeed it is, (answered Finetta,) ‘ come and see yourselves; my eyes are dazzled with ‘ the splendor.’ Whereupon Love’s-Flower climed up, and when she saw the castle, was amazed; and for Fair-Night, whose curiosity did not fail to prompt her to get up in her turn, she seemed as much overjoyed as her sisters. ‘ We must, without dispute (said they) go to ‘ this palace; who knows but we may meet with fine ‘ princes that will think themselves happy to marry us?’ In this manner of discourse they passed away the whole night, when Love’s Flower perceiving Finetta asleep, said to Fair-Night, ‘ Let us dress ourselves in the clothes ‘ Finetta has brought along with her.’ ‘ The thought’s ‘ very good,’ replied Fair-Night. Whereupon they got up and dressed themselves, and made themselves as fine as gold and silver, and jewels could do.

Finetta, who knew not what her sisters had done, opened her sack with a design to dress herself, but how great was her surprise and affliction, when she found nothing but flints and stones? And perceiving at that very juncture her two sisters as bright as the sun in her clothes, she cried and complained of their treachery; who only laughed at her. ‘ How can you (said she to ‘ them) carry me along with you to the castle, with- ‘ out letting me be dressed as well as yourselves.’—‘ We ‘ have but clothes enough for ourselves, (replied Love’s- ‘ Flower) and if thou importunest us thus, thou shalt ‘ feel our blows. ‘ But (continued the other) they are ‘ my own, my god-mother gave them to me, and you ‘ have nothing to do with them.’ ‘ If you teaze us ‘ any longer (said they) we will kill you, and bury you, ‘ and nobody shall know what is become of you.’ Which struck such awe upon poor Finetta, that she durst not

provoke

provoke them, but followed them like their servant-maid,
at a diftance.   The nearer they came to the houfe, the
more wonderful it appeared. ' I cannot but think,
' (faid they one to another) how we fhall be diverted
' and entertained; we fhall eat at the king's table; but
' for Finetta, fhe fhall wafh the difhes in the kitchen;
' and if we are afked who fhe is, let us not make the
' leaft mention of her as our fifter, but fay fhe is a poor
' herdfman's daughter,'—which caft Finetta into defpair, fhe being a girl endowed with wit and beauty.
When they arrived at the gates of the caftle, they knocked very hard, and were let in by a frightful old woman:
She was fifteen feet high, and thirty about, had but one
eye, and that placed in the midft of her forehead, like a
Cyclops, and as large as five others; her nofe was flat,
her fkin black, and her mouth fo large that it was very
frightful. ' Oh! unfortunate creatures, (faid fhe)
' what brought you hither? Do you know that this is
' a giant's caftle, who would eat you all up for his break-
' faft? But it is well he is not at home; I am better
' than he: I will eat but one of you at a time, and you
' will have the comfort of living two or three days lon-
' ger.'   When they heard the giantefs fpeak thus, they
ran away as faft as they could, thinking to fave themfelves; but fhe ftrid as far at one ftep as they at five, and
foon caught them again; and taking one by the hair of
the head, and the others by the arms and necks, threw
them all together into a cave, where there were nought
but toads, fnakes, and the bones of devoured perfons.
And as fhe was then for eating Finetta, and was only
gone for fome oil and vinegar, the giant came: but
thinking to keep them for herfelf, as a nice bit, fhe put
them under a great tub, where they had no light but
through a little hole.
     The giant who was fix times as big as his wife, when
he fpoke made the houfe fhake again, and when he cough-
ed, it feemed like thunder: he had but one large eye,
and his hair was like briftles; he leaned on a piece of
timber, which he ufed for a cane, and held a bafket in
his hand, out of which he took fifteen little children he
                                                         had

had taken away from their parents, and swallowed them like poached eggs. When the three princesses beheld this, they shuddered, but durst not cry, for fear they should be heard, the giant said to his wife, ' I smell ' fresh flesh: give it me.' ' You always fancy, (said ' she) that you smell fresh meat, 'tis nothing but some ' sheep that are going by.' ' Oh! (said the giant) I ' am not to be deceived thus; I am sure I smell fresh ' flesh, and will look for it.' ' Ay do,' replied she, ' And if I find any, (said he) that you have concealed ' from me, I'll cut off your head.' Frightened at this menace, she said to him, ' Be not angry my dear, and ' I will tell you the truth; I have got three young girls, ' that came here to day; but it is a pity to eat them; ' for they know how to do every thing, and as I am ' old, will be very serviceable to me. You know our ' house is very much out of order, our bread is not well ' baked, nor our beer well brewed, and I appear not so ' handsome since I have slaved myself with working; ' they shall be our servants, therefore do not eat them ' now; but if you have a great desire to them at any ' other time, you shall have them.' The giant, with great reluctancy, promised her not to eat them all three, but pressed hard for two; which she opposing, he then desired one of them; which she not acquiesing with, after great disputes he promised her not to eat them; for she designed, when he was gone abroad, to feast herself with them, and to pretend that they had made their escape.

The giant ordered his wife to bring them to him, at which they, poor creatures, were ready to die with fear; but the giantess encouraged them. When he saw them, he asked them what they could do? They answered, That they knew how to clean a house, and sew and spin, and make some ragouts, that all that tasted of them generally licked their plates clean; and that for making of bread, cakes, and patty-pans, they were famous. ' Well, well, (said the giant, who loved a dainty bit) ' make good your words; but, (said he to Finetta) how ' do you know when the oven is hot enough?' ' I lay

' some

' fome butter on it, fir, (replied fhe) and tafte it with
' my tongue.' Thereupon he ordered her to heat the
oven, and the princefs made a terrible fire; for you
muft know, the giant's oven was as large as a ftable, and
he and his wife devoured as much bread as an army;
and the giant, who everlooked them, eat an hundred
cakes and piggins of milk. Love's Flower and Fair-Night
prepared the pafte: the giant faid the oven was hot
enough: Finetta told him, fhe would fee whether it was
fo, and throwing fome pounds of butter into the oven's
mouth, told nim it muft be tafted with the tongue, but
that fhe was too little to do it. ' Oh! (faid he) I am big
' enough.' And thereupon he thruft himfelf fo far in,
that he could not get back again; but was burnt to afhes.

When the giant's wife came to the oven, fhe was furprifed to find fuch a heap of afhes as proceeded from her burnt
hufband. Love's-Flower and Fair-Night, who faw her
very much grieved, did what they could to comfort her;
but at the fame time, were afraid her forrow would be
too foon over, and her appetite come upon her. ' Ma-
' dam, (faid they) have courage, fome king, or great
' prince, will think themfelves happy to marry you.'
Which made her laugh, and fhew her long teeth, that
were as large as a finger. When they faw her in a good
humour, Finetta faid to her, ' If you throw off thefe
' bear fkins, with which you now clothe yourfelf, we will
' drefs you a-la-mode, and you fhall appear as bright
' as any ftar.' ' Let me fee, (faid fhe) what you
' would be at; but affure yourfelf, that if any ladies
' look better than me, I will make mince meat of you.'
Whereupon the three princeffes pulled of her cap, and
combed and frizzled her hair; and while the two fifters
were amufing her after that manner, Finetta with a
hatchet, fevered her head from her body at one blow.

Never was joy equal to their's; they ran up to the top
of the houfe to ring the golden bells, went into all the
chambers of pearls and diamonds, the furniture of which
was fo rich, that it was ecftafy to behold it. They laughed
and fung all that day long, and almoft glutted themfelves
with fweetmeats and other danties. Love's-Flower and

6   Fair-Night

Fair-Night laid in beds of brocade and velvet, and said one to another, ' Our father was never so rich in all his ' prosperity; but yet we want husbands, and may be ' assured nobody will ever come here, since this house ' passes for a place of destruction, since the giant and ' his wife's death are unknown; therefore we must go ' to the next village to shew ourselves in our finery, and ' we shall not be long before we find persons enough ' who will be glad to marry princesses.'

As soon as they were dressed, they told Finetta they were going a-walking, and that she must stay there to take care of the house, and have every thing in order against they returned, or else they should make her feel their blows. When they were gone, Finetta, who was forced to scour and wash, was so overpowered with grief, that she burst out a-crying. ' How unhappy was I, (said she ' to herself) to disobey my godmother! all misfortunes ' have since attended me; my sisters have robbed me of ' my fine clothes, and dressed themselves in them. ' Had it not been for me, the giant and his wife had ' yet been alive; and what am I the better for their ' deaths; I should have been as well pleased to have ' been devoured by them, as to live as I do now.' When she had said all this, she cried so much, that her eyes were almost swoln out of her head; and when her sisters came, she had the mortification to see them bring with them oranges, and sweetmeats, and fine fruits, and to hear them tell what respect they had paid by a king's son at a ball they had been at; and withal, to be bid to come and undress them, and lay up their clothes; which she durst not refuse; for if ever she complained, they flew upon her, and beat her till they had left her for dead.

The next day they went again, and came back as before, and lived in that manner some time; when one night as Finetta was sitting over a handful of fire, not knowing what to do with herself, raking among the cinders, she found an old rusty cankered key; and after having taking a great deal of pains to scour it, found it to be gold, and thinking it might open some lock in the

house.

houfe, tried them all, and it belonged to a fine box, which
fhe opened, wherein there were rich clothes, diamonds,
laces, fine linen, ribbons, and things of great value.
Never mentioning a word of this good fortune, fhe waited impatiently for her fifters going a gain the next day;
and then as foon as fhe faw them out of doors, dreffed
herfelf fo fine, that fhe appeared as fine as the fun, and
went to the fame ball; and though fhe had no mafk on,
yet her clothes had made fo great an alteration in her for
the better, that they did not know her. When fhe appeared in that affembly, there was heard a murmuring
of voices, fome out of admiration, and others of jealoufy;
and when fhe danced, fhe excelled as much therein as in
her beauty.

Love's-Flower and Fair-Night, who had made there
ftrange havock among the hearts, feeing the favourable
reception this ftranger met with, were ready to burft with
jealoufy: but Finetta, who behaved herfelf extraordinary well, feemed by her air, as if fhe was made to command. Love's-Flower and Fair-Night, who had been
ufed to fee their fifter dirty and grimy, retained fo
fmall an idea of her face, that they knew her not, but
paid as much refpect to her as the reft; and fhe, as foon
as the ball was over, ran home as faft as fhe could, and
put on her dirty rags again. When her fifters came
home, they told her they had feen a charming young
princefs, whofe fkin was as white as fnow, the colour of
her cheeks as frefh as a rofe, her teeth as even and as
white as ivory, and for her lips they looked like coral,
and that her clothes were all of gold and diamonds.
This fport continued fome time, and Finetta every ball
appeared in a different drefs; for the cheft was inexhauftible, and the clothes were all fo fafhionable, that
the ladies followed that mode.

One night that Finetta had danced very much, and
had ftaid longer than ordinary, and was willing to get
home foon enough, that fhe might not be difcovered by
her fifters, fhe made fo much hafte, that fhe loft her flipper, which was of red velvet, braided with pearls, and was
found the next day by the prince of Chery, the king's
                                                    eldeft

eldeſt ſon, as he was hunting, and admired it ſo much
for its ſmallneſs, that he kiſſed it, and carried it home
with him ; and from that day, grew ſo melancholy, and
reſerved, that he never would ſpeak, loſt his ſtomach, fell
away, and looked ſo ill, that the king and queen, who
loved him to diſtraction, ſent for all the remedies and
aſſiſtance they could get ; but all to no purpoſe, for the
phyſicians, after they had conſulted together, and made
their obſervations for two or three days together, con-
cluded that he was in love, and would die unleſs he had
ſome relief.

The queen, who doated on him, cried day and night
over him : but could make no diſcovery who the beloved perſon was.   She brought all the moſt beautiful
. ladies of the court into his chamber, but he would not ſo
much as look at them.   At laſt, the queen ſaid to him
one day. ‘ My dear child, you overwhelm us with
‘ grief ; we know you are in love, wherefore then ſhould
‘ you hide it from us ? Tell who the lovely perſon is,
‘ and ſhould ſhe prove a ſhepherdeſs, we will not oppoſe
‘ your deſires.’   Hereupon the prince grown more bold
by the queen’s promiſes, pulled the ſlipper from under
his bolſter ; ‘ This madam (ſaid he) is the cauſe of my
‘ illneſs ; I found this pretty little ſlipper as I was one
‘ day a-hunting, and am reſolved never to marry any
‘ but the perſon who can draw it on.’   ‘ Alas ! child,
‘ (ſaid the queen) grieve not, we ſhall ſoon find her out.’
And then ſhe left them, and told the king, who was very
much ſurpriſed at the ſtrangeneſs of his paſſion, and
ordered to be proclaimed by ſound of trumpet, That all
women ſhould come and try on the ſlipper, and that
the perſon whom it fitted ſhould be married to the prince.

Upon this, all the fine ladies of the court waſhed and
paired their feet, and made choice of the thinneſt
ſtockings, that they might put on the ſlipper ; but all to
no purpoſe, ſince none of them could get it on ; which
was no ſmall affliction to the prince.   Love’s-Flower and
Fair-Night, upon this, dreſſed themſelves ſo fine one
day, that Finetta was amazed, and aſked them where
they were going ? Who told her, to court, to try on the
                                                 ſlipper

flipper that the king's fon had found, and that whoever
fucceeded, was to marry him. Whereupon Finetta afked,
if fhe might not go? Which made them laugh at her,
and tell her, they wondered how fuch a dirty girl as
fhe could have any fuch thoughts, bidding her water
the garden, for fhe was fit for nothing elfe.

When they were gone, Finetta had a great mind to
try her fortune, having a ftrong fancy of her fuccefs;
but was fomething at a lofs, becaufe fhe knew not the
way: for the ball fhe was at before was not kept at court.
However, fhe dreffed herfelf very magnificently, her
gown was of blue fattin, covered over with ftars of diamonds; a full moon was placed in the middle of her
back, and a fun upon her head, which gave fuch a luftre,
as dazzled the eyes of the fpectators. When fhe opened
the door to go out, fhe was very much furprifed to find
the Spanifh horfe there; fhe carreffed him, and was overjoyed to fee him, and mounted on him, appeared a thoufand times more beautiful than Helen. The horfe went
prancing along, and by the noife he made with champ-
ing of his bits, made Love's-Flower and her fifter look
behind, to fee who was coming after them; but how
great was their aftonifhment, when they faw it was
Finetta! ' I proteft, (faid Love's Flower to Fair Night)
' 'tis Finetta;' and the other was about to make fome
reply, when the horfe paffing by, dafhed them all over
with dirt; whereupon Finetta told them, that fhe defpifed them as they deferved, and fo put forward.
' Certainly, (faid Fair-Night) we dream; who could
' have furnifhed her with this horfe and fine cloaths?
' 'Tis a miracle to me: fhe will, without difpute, have
' the good fortune to get the flipper, therefore 'tis in
' vain for us to go any farther.'

While they were in the utmoft rage and defpair, Finetta arrived at the palace, where fhe being taken for a
queen, the guards were under arms, with drums beating
and trumpets founding. She went into the prince's
chamber, who no fooner fet his eyes on her, but he was
charmed, and wifhed her foot fmall enough to put on
                                                    the

the flipper; which fhe not only did do, but alfo produced
the fellow to it.　Upon which all perfons prefent cried,
Long live the Princefs; and the prince arofe from off his
bed, came and kiffed her hand, and declared to her his
paffion.　As foon as the king and queen heard of it,
they came overjoyed; the queen flung her arms about
her neck, and embraced her. and called her daughter.
The king and queen made her great prefents, the can-
nons were fired, and there were the moft public demonftrations of joy poffible.

The prince defired fhe would confent to his happinefs, and that they might be married; which fhe refufed till fhe had told him her adventures, which fhe did in
a few words.　Their joy was augmented fo much the
more, when they knew her to be a princefs by birth;
and, upon acquainting them with the names of her father and mother, informed her that they had deprived
them of their kingdoms.　As foon as fhe knew that, fhe
vowed never to give her hand to the prince, unlefs they
were reftored again to their dominions, which the king
her father-in-law made no fcruple to grant.　In the mean
time, Love's-Flower and Fair-Night arrived, and the
firft news they heard, was, that their fifter had put on
the flipper, and were fo much confufed, that they knew
not what to fay or do; but at laft were for going back
again; when fhe hearing that they were there, fent for
them, and, inftead of ufing them as they deferved, met
them, and embraced them, afterwards prefented them
to the queen, acquainted her that they were her fifters,
for whom fhe defired fhe would have fome refpect.
They were fo much furprifed at their fifter's goodnefs,
that they ftood fpeechlefs; but, upon her telling them
that the prince her fpoufe would reftore the king their
father, and fend them into their own country, they fell
on their knees before her, and wept for joy.

·The nuptials were celebrated with all the pomp imaginable; Finetta writ a letter to her god-mother, which
fhe fent with great prefents by the Spanifh horfe, defiring
her to find out the king and queen her father and mother, and let them know her good fortune, that they
might

return to their own kingdoms; which commiſſion the fairy acquitted herſelf of, and the king and queen were reſtored to their dominions. Love's-Flower and Fair-Night lived as great and happy as they could deſire, and became afterwards great queens, as well as their ſiſter.

The Morality of this Tale is, that while we act conſiſtently with virtuous Principles, however Misfortunes may attend, yet in the End, Happineſs will ſucceed; and ſuch as are good will ever meet a juſt Reward.

THE STORY

OF THE

WHITE CAT.

THERE was a king who had three ſons, all handſome, brave young gentlemen; but jealous that they ſhould deſire to reign before his death, he cauſed ſeveral reports to be ſpread abroad, that they endeavoured to procure themſelves creatures to deprive him of his crown. The king found himſelf very old, but his ſenſe and capacity of government no ways decayed; ſo that he cared not to reſign up a place he filled ſo worthily, and thought that the beſt way for him to live at
quiet,

quiet, was to amufe them by promifes. To this end
he took them into his clofet, where, after he had talked
to them with great candour, he faid, ' You will agree
' with me, my children, that my great age will not al-
' low me to apply myfelf to the affairs of the public
' with as much care as formerly; and I am afraid my
' fubjects will not be fo well pleafed with my adminif-
' tration. Therefore I intend to refign my crown to
' one of you. But as it is very juft that you fhould
' ftrive to pleafe me with fuch a prefent, and as I defign
' to retire into the country, I fhould be very glad to
' have a pretty little dog to keep me company, there-
' fore, without having more regard to my eldeft than
' my youngeft, I declare to you, that he of you who
' brings me the moft beautiful dog, fhall be my heir.'

The three princes were very much furprifed at their
father's defire for a little dog. For the two younger,
they were extraordinarily well pleafed at this propofal;
and for the elder, he was either too timorous or refpectful to reprefent his right. However they took their
leaves of the king, who gave them money and jewels,
telling them, that they muft all return without fail in a
year's time, on a certain day with the dogs. But before
they fet out on this fearch, they all went to a caftle, three
leagues off, where they made an entertainment, and
invited their moft trufty friends and confidants, before
whom the three brothers fwore an eternal friendfhip to
one another, promifing never to be jealous of each others
good fortune; but that the moft fuccefsful fhould let
the other two partake with him, appointing that caftle
for their place of rendezvous, and from thence to go all
together to the king.

They every one took a different road without any
attendants; and for the two eldeft, they had a great
many adventures: but as the particulars are not fo well
known to me, I fhall pafs them over in filence, and
fpeak only of the youngeft, who was a prince of a fweet
behaviour, exact fhape, fine features, had delicate teeth,
performed all exercifes fit for a prince with a good grace;
and to fum up all in one, was a youth of bright parts,
and

and brave even, to a fault: befides he fang very agreeably, and played on the lute and the orbo to admiration,
and painted with great judgment. Not a day paffed
over his head, but he bought dogs of fome kind or other,
as hounds, grey-hounds, fpaniels, &c. that were pretty,
keeping always the moft beautiful, and letting the others
go; for it was impoffible for him to keep all the dogs
he had purchafed, fince he had neither gentleman, page,
nor any other perfon along with him: however, he kept
going on, without fixing on any certain place: when he
was furprifed one night in a large foreft, where he could
find no fhelter, by a ftorm of thunder, lightning, and
rain. Still he purfued the road, and went a long way,
when feeing a fmall light, he perfuaded himfelf fome
houfe was nigh, where he might get a lodging that night.
Following the lights, he arrived at the gates of a ftately
caftle, which were all of maffy gold; in which were re-
flectors which gave that extraordinary light which the
prince faw fo far off. The walls were of fine china,
whereon the hiftories of all the Fairies fince the creation
of the world were reprefented; but the rain and ill-wea-
ther would not fuffer our prince to ftay to examine them
all, though he was charmed to find the adventures of
prince Lutin, who was his uncle among the reft.

He returned to the door, after having rambled fome
paces off, and there found a deer's foot at the end of a
chain of diamonds, which made him admire the magnificence: he pulled, and foon heard a bell, which by the
found, he judged to be either gold or filver; and fome
time after the door opened, and he faw no perfon, but
only twelve hands, each hold a flambeau; at which fight
he was very much furprifed, and was in difpute whether
or no he fhould proceed any farther, when, to his great
amazement he felt fome others behind him, which pufhed
him forwards; whereupon he advanced with his hand
on his fword, though very uneafy, and, as he thought, in
fome danger: when going into a wardrobe of por-
phyry and lapis lazuli, he heard two fweet voices fing
thefe words:

With

With unconcern behold thofe hands,
- And dread no falfe alarms,
If you are fure you can withftand
· The force of beauty's charms.

He could not believe he was invited fo kindly to fuffer any injury, which made him, finding himfelf forced
forwards, to go to a great gate of coral, which opened as
foon as he approached it, and he went into a hall of mother o'pearl, and thence into feveral chambers adorned
and enriched with paintings and jewels: a vaft number
of lights that were let down from the cieling of the hall,
contributed to light fome part of the other apartments,
which befides were hung round with glafs fconces.   In
fhort, the magnificence was almoft incredible.   After
having gone into fixty chambers, the hand that conducted him ftopt him, and he faw a great eafy chair
make up towards him; the fire lit of itfelf, and the
hands, which were both white and finely proportioned,
undrefs'd him, he being wet, and in fome danger of catch-
ing cold.   A fine fhirt and a night-gown of gold brocade, with cyphers and fmall emeralds, were given him,
and a table and toilet brought by thefe hands.   Every
thing was very grand: the hands comb'd out his hair
with a lightnefs that gave him pleafure, and afterwards
dreffed him in extraordinary fine cloaths, while he not
only filently admired them, but at laft began to be in
fome little fright.   When he was dreffed that he feemed
as beautiful as Adonis, they conducted him into a ftately
hall richly furnifhed, where he faw in a fine painting,
the ftories of the moft famous cats; as Rodillardus hung
by the heels in a council of rats, the Cat in Boots, the
Marquis de Corabus the Writing Cat, the Cat turn'd
Woman, Witches in the fhape of Cats, with their night-
ly meetings, &c. all very odd and fingular.

Two cloths were laid, both garnifhed with gold plate,
with beaufets fet out with vaft numbers of glaffes, and
cups made of valuable ftones; and while the prince was
thinking with himfelf, what they were laid for, be faw
fome cats come and place themfelves upon a bench fet
there

for that purpose, one holding a music-book, another with a roll of paper, to beat time with, and the rest with small guittars: when all on a sudden, they every one set up a mewing in different tones, and struck the strings with their talons, which made the strangest music that ever was heard. The prince would have thought himself in hell, if the palace had not been so wonderful fine, it put him so much in mind of it; then stopping his ears, he laughed heartily at the several postures and grimaces of these strange musicians. And while he was calling to mind the several things that had happened since his being in this castle, he saw a little figure about half a yard high came forward in a vale of black crape, led by two cats in mourning cloaks, with swords by their sides, and followed by a numerous train of cats; some carrying rats, and some mice in traps and cages.

The prince was in the greatest amazement, and knew not what to think; when the little figure in black coming up to him, and lifting up its veil, he saw the prettiest little white cat he ever had set his eyes on, which seemed to be young, but withal very melancholy, and set up such an agreeable mewing, as went to the prince's heart. Prince, (said she) you are welcome; ' it is a pleasure to me to see you here.' ' Madam ' Puss, (replied the prince) you are very generous to ' receive me so graciously; but you appear to me to ' be a cat of extraordinary merit: for the gift you have ' of speech, and this stately castle you possess, are con- ' vincing proofs of it.' ' Prince, (answered the White ' Cat) I desire you would forbear your compliments, ' for I am both plain in my discourse and manners, ' but have a good heart. Let us go, (said she) to sup- ' per, and bid the musicians leave off, for the prince does ' not understand what they say.' What, (said he) do ' they then say any thing?' ' Yes, (answered the White ' Cat) we have poets, and great wits, and if you will ' stay with us, you shall be convinced of it. ' I need ' but hear you speak to believe that, (answered he, gal- ' lantly) for I look on you as on something more than ' common.'

Supper was brought up, the hands set on the table two dishes of soup, one made of young pigeons, and the other of fat mice. The sight of the one hindred the prince from eating the other, fancying that the same cook had dressed both; which the White Cat guessed at, assured him that she had two kitchens, and that he might eat of whatever was set before him, and be confident there were no rats or mice in any thing offered him. The prince, who believed that this beautiful cat would not deceive him, wanted not to be told so twice. He observed a little picture to hang upon her foot, at which he was not a little surprised and asked her to shew it him, thinking it might be some fine puss, a lover of the White Cat; but was in a maze to see a handsome young man, who resembled him very much. The White Cat sighed, and growing melancholy, kept a profound silence. The prince perceiving that there was something extraordinary in it, but durst not inform himself for fear of displeasing or grieving his kind entertainer. He diverted her with all the news he knew, and found her well acquainted with the different interests of princes, and other things that passed in the world. When supper was done, the White Cat carried her guest into a hall, where there was a stage, on which twelve cats, and as many apes, danced a mask in Moorish and Chinese habits; and when this was over, the White Cat bid her guest good-night, and the hands led him into an apartment opposite to that which he had seen, but no less magnificent: It was hung with tapestry, made of the wings of butterflies, the variety of which colours formed most beatiful flowers. The bed was of fine gauze, tied with bunches of ribbon, and the glasses reached from the cieling down to the floor, and the pannels between represented, in carved work, thousands of cupids.

The prince went to bed, and slept a little; but was awakened again by a confused noise. The hands took him out of bed, and put on him a hunting habit. He looked out of the window, and saw above five hundred cats, some leading greyhounds, and others blowing horns!

.it

it being that day a great feaſt, whereon the White Cat
had a mind to go a hunting, and was willing that the
prince ſhould partake of that diverſion.   The hands
preſented to him a wooden horſe, that had a good ſpeed
and eaſy paces, which he made ſome ſcruple to mount,
alledging, they took him for Don Quixotte; but his re-
fuſal ſignified nothing, they ſet him on the wooden horſe,
which was finely capariſoned, with a ſaddle and houſing
of gold, beſet with diamonds.   The White Cat rid on a
moſt beautiful ape, having thrown off her veil, and put
on a hat and feather, which gave her ſo bold an air,
as frightened all the mice that ſaw her.   Never was
there better ſport; the cats out-run the mice and
rabbits, and whenever they took one, the White
Cat always paunch'd its pray, and gave them
their fees.   For the birds they were not in much greater
ſecurity; the cats climb'd the trees, and the ape carried
the White Cat up to the eagles neſts.   When the chaſe
was over, ſhe took a horn of about a finger's length,
which, when ſounded, was ſo loud, that it might be
heard ſome leagues; and as ſoon as ſhe blowed, ſhe had
preſently all the cats in the country about her, ſome
mounted in chariots in the air, and ſome in boats, but
all in different habits, which made a fine ſhow.   With
this pompous train ſhe and the prince returned to her
caſtle, who thought it favored very much of ſorcery;
but was more ſurpriſed at the cat's ſpeaking than all
the reſt.

As ſoon as ſhe came home, ſhe put on her black veil
again, and ſupped with the prince, whom the freſh air
had got a good ſtomach; the hands brought him fine
liquors, which he not only drank off with pleaſure, but
made him forget the little dog he was to procure for his
father: his thoughts were bent on bearing the White
Cat company, and he ſpent his time in hunting and
fiſhing, and ſometimes in balls and plays.   The White
Cat made ſuch paſſionate ſongs and verſes, that he began to think ſhe had a tender heart, ſince ſhe could not
expreſs herſelf as ſhe did, and be inſenſible of the power
of love, but her ſecretary, who was an old cat, wrote
ſo bad a hand, that ſhould any of her works remain, it

E 2   would

would be impoffible to read them.   The prince had forgot his country, the hand ftill waited on him, and he
regretted his not being a cat, that he might pafs his life
in fuch pleafant company.   ' Alas! (faid he to the
' White Cat) how forry am I to leave you, fince I love
' you dearly!   Either become a woman, or change me
' into a cat.'   Which wifh the White Cat only anfwered in obfcure words, though fhe was mightily pleafed
with it.

    Thus a year flipt away free from care and pain.
The White Cat knew the time he was to return, and as
he did not think of it, put him in mind thereof.   ' Don't
' you know, (faid fhe) that you have but three days to
' find a litt'e dog in, and that your brothers have got
' fome very fine ones?'   This rouzed the prince out of
his lethargy: ' By what fecret charm, (cried he) have
' I forgot the only thing in the world, that is of the
' greateft importance to me?   What will become of my
' honour and fortune?   Where fhall I find a little dog
' beautiful enough to gain a kingdom, and a horfe
' fwift enough to make diligent fearch after one?'
Then beginning to afflict himfelf, and grew uneafy, the
White Cat faid to him, ' Do not grieve, prince, I am
' your friend; you may ftay here a day longer yet;
' for though it is five hundred leagues off, the good
' wooden horfe will carry you there in lefs than twelve
' hours.'   ' I thank you beautiful Cat, (faid he) but
' 'tis not enough for me to return to my father; I muft
' carry with me a little dog.'   ' Here, take this acorn,
' (faid the White Cat) it has a beautiful little dog in
' it; put it to your ear, and you will hear it bark.'
The prince obeyed, heard it bark, and was tranfported
with joy. he would have opened it, fo great was his curiofity; but the White Cat told him it might catch cold,
and he had better ftay till he gave it to his father.   He
thanked her a thoufand times, and bid her a tender
farewell, affuring her that he never paffed his days fo
pleafantly as with her, and that he was grieved to leave
her behind him: adding, that though fhe was a fovereign,
and had great court paid to her, yet he could not
                                            forbear

forbear afking her to go along with him: to which po-
pofition fhe anfwered only with a figh.

The prince came firft to the caftle, that was appointed for the rendezvous with his brothers, who arrived foon
after, but were very much furprifed to fee a wooden
horfe in the court, that leaped better than any in the
academies. The prince went to meet them; they embraced, and gave each other an account of their adventures; but our prince took care to conceal the truth of
his, and fhewed them only an ugly turntpit, telling them
that he thought him very pretty: At which, though they
were very good friends, the two eldeft conceived a fecret
joy. The next day they all three went in the fame
coach to the king. The two eldeft carried their dogs in
bafkets fo white and delicate, that none durft hardly
touch them; and the youngeft had his poor defpicable
turnfpit in a ftring. When they came to the palace,
the courtiers crowded about them to welcome them home.
The king, when they came into his apartment, knew
not in whofe favour to declare, for the two little dogs
that the elder brothers brought were almoft of equal
beauty, when the youngeft pulling the acorn out of his
pocket, which the White Cat give him, put an end to
the difference. As foon as he opened it, they all faw a
little dog laid on cotton, and fo fmall, that he might go
through a ring without touching it. The prince fat it
on the ground, and prefently it began to dance a fara-
band, with caftanets, as nimble and as well as the beft
Spaniard. It was of a mixture of feveral colours, its
ears and long hair reached the ground. The king was
very much furprifed, and thought it was impoffible to
meet with any thing fo beautiful as Tonton, by which
name it was called, yet he was not very ready to part
with his crown, the leaft gem of which, was dearer to
him than all the dogs in the world. He told his children, that he was very well pleafed with the pains they
had taken, but they had fucceeded fo well in the firft
thing he had defired, that he had a mind to make fur-
ther proof of their abilities before he performed his promife: And that was, he would give them a year to find

E 3

out

out a fine web of cloth fine enough to go through the
eye of a small working needle.   They all stood surprised and concerned, that they were to go again upon
another search ; however, the two elder seemed the most
ready, and all three parted with ut making so great a
profession of friendship as they did the first time, for
the story of the turnspit had somewhat abated it.

Our prince mounted his wooden horse again, and
without looking after any other assistance, than what he
might expect from the friendship of the White Cat, returned in all diligence to the castle, where he had been
so well received; where he net only found all the doors
open, but the windows, walls, and walks illuminated.
The hands came and met him, held his horse's bridle,
and led him into the stable, while the prince went to
the White Cat's chamber, who was laid in a little
basket, on a quilt of white sattin.   When she saw the
prince, she made a thousand skips and jumps, to express
her joy, and said, ' Whatever reason I might have,
' Prince, to hope for your return, I must own I durst
' not flatter myself with it; since I am generally un-
' happy in what I most desire, therefore this surprises
' me.'   The prince, full of acknowledgement, caressed
her often, and told her the success he had in his journey,
which she was not unacquainted with, and that the king
required a web of cloth so fine, as it might be drawn
through the eye of a needle, which he believed was a
thing impossible; but that however he would not fail to
try to procure such a one, relying on her friendship and
assistance.   The White Cat, putting on a grave air,
told him it was an affair that required some considera-
tion, that by good fortune she had in her castle some
cats that spun very fine, that she would do what she
could to forward that work, so that he might stay there,
and not trouble himself to search elsewhere, it being
unlikely for him to meet with any so easily.

Soon after the hands appeared, carrying flambeaux,
and the prince followed the White Cat into a Magnificent gallery that looked on to a river, upon which there
were some artificial fire-works, made to burn four cats,
who

who had been accused and convicted of eating some
roast-meat, designed for the White Cat's supper; with
some cheese and milk; and besides, for conspiring against
her person with Martifax and Lermites, two famous
rats in that country: But as it was thought that there
was a great deal of injustice done them, and that most
of the witnesses were suborned, the prince obtained their
pardon; notwithstanding, the fire-works were let off,
which gave the prince very great diversion.   Afterwards a genteel repast was served up, which gave the
prince more pleasure than the fire, for his riding had
got him an extraordinary stomach: For the rest of the
time, he spent it in agreeable entertainments, with
which the ingenious White Cat diverted her guests, who
was perhaps the first mortal that was so well entertained
by cats without any other company.   Indeed the White
Cat had a ready wit, and could discourse on any sub-
ject, which often put the prince into a great consterna-
tion, and made him say to her, ' Certainly, all this
' that I observe so wonderful in you, cannot be natural;
' therefore tell me by what prodigy you think and speak
' so justly?' Forbear asking me any questions, prince,
' (said she) for I am n t allowed to answer them, but
' you may conjecture what you please; let it suffice
' that I have used you with respect, and that I interest
' myself tenderly in what regards you.'

The second year rolled away insensibly, as well as the
first: the prince wished for nothing, but the diligent
hands brought to him, whether books, jewels, fine pictures, or antique medals, &c. when the White Cat, who
was always watchful for the prince's interest, informed
him that the time of his departure drew nigh: but that
he might be easy concerning the web of cloth, for she
had a wonderful fine one made; and added withal, that
this time she would give him an equipage suitable to his
birth, and without waiting for an answer, obliged him
to look into the great court of the castle, in which there
waited an open chariot of embossed work in gold, in
several gallant devices, drawn by twelve milk-white
horses, four a-breast, whose harnesses were covered with

E   velvet

velvet of fire-colour, which was the fame as the lining of
the chariot, befet with diamonds, and the buckles of
gold.   An hundred coaches with eight horfes, full of the
lords of his retinue, magnificently cloathed, followed his
chariot, which was guarded befides by a thoufand body-
guards, whofe cloathing was fo full of embroidery, that
the cloth was hardly difcovered; and what is very fingular, the White Cat's picture was feen every where, both
in the devices on the chariot, and on the guards.   ' Go,
' prince, (faid fhe) and appear at the king your father's
' court, in fo ftately a manner, that your magnificence
' may ferve to impofe on him, that he may refufe you
' no longer the crown you deferve.   Take this walnut,
' be fure to crack it in his prefence, and you will find in
' it fuch a web as you want.'   ' Lovely White Cat,
' (faid he) I own I am fo penetrated with your bounty,
' that if you will give your confent I will prefer paffing
' my days with you, before all the grandeur I may pro-
' mife myfelf elfewhere.'   ' Prince (replied fhe) I am
' perfuaded of the kindnefs of your heart, which is a
' rare thing among princes, who would be refpected by
' all the world, and love none but themfelves; but you
' fhew me this rule is not general.   I make great account
' of the attachment you have for a little White Cat,
' that in the main is fit for nothing but to catch mice.'
At that the prince kiffed her paw, and went away.

It is almoft incredible to believe the hafte he made,
were we unacquainted with the fwiftnefs of the wooden
horfe, who carried him before five hundred thoufand
leagues in lefs than two days; and the fame power that
animated him, had fo great an effect upon the others,
that he was not above four-and-twenty hours upon the
road, and never ftopt till he arrived at the king's palace,
where his two brothers had got before him; who feeing
he was not come, rejoiced at his negligence, and faid to
one another, ' How fortunate is this? he is either fick
' or dead, and will not come to rival us in this impor-
' tant bufinefs.'   Thereupon they pulled out their webs;
which were indeed very fine, and paffed them through
the eye of a large needle, but not a fmall one; which

                                                    pretext

pretext of refusal the king embracing, went and fetched the needle he proposed, which the magistrates, by his order, had carried to the treasury, and locked up carefully: This refusal raised a great murmuring: Those that were friends to the princes, and particularly the eldest, whose web was the finest, said it was all a trick and evasion: And the king's creatures maintained, that he was not obliged to keep any, other conditions than what were proposed; when, to put an end to this difference, there was heard a sounding of trumpets and hautboys, which came before our prince.

The king and his sons were all surprised at this magnificence. The prince, after he had respectfully saluted his father, and embraced his brothers, took out of his box, covered with rubies, a walnut which he cracked, thinking to find the web so much boasted of; but only saw a small hazel nut, which he cracked also, and to his surprise found only a kernel of wax. The king and every body laughed, to think that the prince had been so credulous as to think to carry a web of cloth in a nut: but had they recollected themselves, they might have remembered the little dog that lay in an acorn. However he peeled the kernel, and nothing appeared but the pulp itself, whereupon a great noise was heard all over the room, every one having it in his mouth what a fool the prince was made of; who, for his part, returned no answer to all the pleasantries of the courtiers, but broke the kernel, and found in it a corn of wheat, and in that a grain of millet. At the sight of this he began to distrust, and muttered to himself, ' O ' White Cat! White Cat! thou hast deceived me! And at that Instant he felt a cat's paw upon his hand, which scratched him, and fetched blood; he knew not whether it was to encourage or dismay him. However, he opened the millet feed, and to the amazement of all present, drew out a web of cloth, four hundred yards long! and what was more wonderful, there were painted on it all forts of birds, beasts and fish; fruits, trees and plants; rocks, and all manner of rare shells of the sea; the sun, moon, stars and planets; and all the pictures of all the kings and princes of the world, with those of their wives, mistresses and children, all dressed after the fashion of

E 5   their

their own country. When the king saw this piece of cloth, he turned as pale as the prince was red in looking so long for it, and the needle was brought, and it was put through five or six times; all which time, the king and his two sons were silent, though afterwards, the beauty and rarity of the cloth was so great, they said it was not to be matched in the whole world. The king fetched a deep sigh, and turning himself towards his children, said to them! ' Nothing gives me so much com-
' fort in my old age, as to be sensible of the deference
' you have for me, which makes me desirous of putting
' you to a new trial. Go and travel another year, and
' he that brings me the most beautiful damsel, shall
' marry her, and be crowned king, there being an ab-
' solute necessity that my successor should marry; and
' I swear and promise. I will no longer defer the re-
' ward.'

Our prince suffered all this injustice; the little dog and the web of cloth rather deserved ten crowns than one; but he was of so sweet a disposition, that he would not thwart his father's will: so without any delay he got into his chariot again, and with his train returned to his dear White Cat, who knowing the day and moment he would come, had the roads strewed with flowers. She was laid on a persian tapestry, under a canopy of cloth of gold, in a gallery from whence she could see him return. He was received by the hands that always served him, and all the cats climed upon the gutter to congratulate his return by a concert of mewing. ' Well,
' prince, (said she to him) I see you are come back
' without your crown.' ' Madam, (replied he) by
' your bounty I was in a condition of gaining it; but I
' am persuaded the king is more loth to part with it
' than I am fond of having it.' No matter for
' that (said she) you must neglect nothing to
' deserve it, I will assist you on this occasion; and
' since you must carry a beautiful damsel to your
' father's court, I will look out for one, who shall gain
' you the prize: but in the interim, let us be merry,
' and divert ourselves. I have ordered a sea-fight be-
' tween may cats and the most terrible rats of the coun-
' try.

'try. My cats perhaps may be hard fet, for they are afraid
'of the water; however, they will have advantage
'enough: we cannot expect it in every thing.' The
prince returned her thanks, and faid feveral very handfome things on her conduct and prudence.   Afterwards they went upon a terrafs which looked on to the
fea.   The cats' veffels confifted of great pieces of cork,
on which they floated very commodioufly: and thefe of
the rats of egg-fhells joined together.   The fight was
very obftinate; the rats threw themfelves into the water,
and fwam better than the cats, infomuch that they as
often conquered, as they were conquered; when Mina-
grobis, the admiral of the cats, reduced the rattifh race
to the utmoft defpair, by eating up the admiral of
their fleet, who was an old experienced rat, that had
made three voyages round the world in very good fhips,
in which he was neither captain nor failor, but only a
kind of interloper.   But the White Cat was fo politic,
that fhe would not abfolutly deftroy thefe poor unfortunate rats, thinking that if there we.e no rats nor
mice, her fubjects would live in an idlenefs that might
become prejudicial to her.

The prince paffed this year, as he had done the two
firft, in hunting, fifhing, and fuch diverfions, and often
at a game of chefs, which the White Cat played extraordinary well at; but he could not forbear often quef-
tioning her, to know by what miracle fhe fpoke.   He
afked her, if fhe was a fairy, or if by any metamorphofis
fhe was turned into a cat.   But as the White Cat was
always capable of faying what fhe had a mind to, fhe
returned him an anfwer fo infignificant, that he perceived fhe was not willing to communicate this fecret
to him.   As nothing paffes away fo quick as happy
days, if the White Cat had not been fo careful as to
remember the time the prince was to return, 'tis certain he would have quite forgot it.   She told him of
it the night before, and withal, that the hour of deftroy-
ing the fatal work of the faries was come; and therefore he muft refolve to cut off her head and tail, and
throw them prefently into the fire.   ' What, (cried he)
                     E 6   ' fhall

'shall I my lovely White Cat, be so barbarous as to
'kill you? you have undoubtedly a mind to make proof
'of my heart, but be assured it is incapable of wanting
'that friendship and acknowledgment due to you.'
'No prince, (continued she) I do not suspect you of
'ingratitude: I know your merit; but neither you nor
'I can prescribe to fate: do what I desire you, we shall
'thereby be happy: and you shall know upon the word
'of a cat of worth and honour, that I am really your
'friend.' Tears started two or three times in the young
prince's eyes, to think he must cut off the head of his
pretty White Cat, that had been so kind to him; he
said all that he could think most tender to engage her
to dispense with him: to which she answered obsti-
nately, she would die by his hand, and that was the
only way to hinder his brother from having the crown.
In short, she pressed him so earnestly, that he trembling, with an unsteady hand, cut off her head and
tail, and threw them presently into the fire; and at
the same time saw the most charming metamorphosis
imaginable. The body of the White Cat grew presently
large, and changed all on a sudden to a fine lady, so
accomplished, as exceeds description. Her eyes committed theft upon all hearts, and her sweetness kept
them: her shape was majestic, her air noble and modest, her wit flowing, her manners engaging; in a word,
she was beyond every thing that was lovely.

The prince, at the sight of her, was in so agreeable
a surprise, that he thought himself enchanted. He
could not speak nor look at her, and his tongue was so
tied, that he could not explain his amazement; which
was much greater, when he saw an extraordinary number of gentlemen, and ladies, holding their cat-skins
over their shoulders, come and prostrate themselves at
the queen's feet, to testify their joy to see her again in
her natural state. She received them with all the
marks of bounty, which sufficiently discovered the sweetness of her temper. After having spent sometime in
hearing their compliments, she ordered them to retire,

and

and leave her alone with the prince; to whom she
spoke as follows.

'.Think not, sir, that I have always been a cat, and
' that my birth is obscure. My father was king of
' six kingdoms, loved my mother tenderly, and gave
' her liberty to do what she pleased. Her most pre-
' vailing inclination was to travel, infomuch that when
' she was with child of me, she undertook to go and see
' a mountain, of which she had heard a most surpris-
' ing account. As she was on the road she was told
' there was, nigh the place she was then at, an ancient
' castle of fairies, which was the finest in the world, or
' at least said to be so; for as no person was ever ad-
' mitted into it, there could not be any positive
' judgment passed thereon: but for the gardens, they
' were known to contain the best fruits that ever were
' eat.   The queen·my mother, who longed to taste
' them, went thither. But when she came to the gate
' of this stately edifice, which shined again with blue,
' enameled with gold; nobody came, though she knocked
' a long time; and her desire increasing the more, by
' reason of the difficulty, she sent for ladders to scale
' the walls: but they growing visibly to a great height
' of themselves, they were forced to fasten the ladders
' to one another, to lengthen them, and whenever any
' one went up them, they broke under their weight;
' so that they were either killed or lamed. The queen
' was in the utmost despair to see trees loaded with
' such delicious fruits, and not to taste of them, which
' she was resolved to do, or die; infomuch that she
' ordered some rich tents to be pitched before the castle,
' and stayed there six weeks, with all her court. She
' neither slept nor eat, but sighed continually, and was
' always talking of the fruit. In short, she fell dan-
' gerously ill, and no remedy could be found out, for
' the inexorable fairies never appeared from the time
' she came there. All her court were very much griev-
' ed: there was nought to be heard but sighs and la-
' mentations, while the dying queen was continually
' asking those that were in waiting upon her, for fruit;
but

‘ but would eat of none but what came out of this gar-
‘ den.

. ‘ One Night, after having got a little fleep, when
‘ fhe awakened fhe faw a little ugly decrepit old wo-
‘ man fit in an elbow chair by her bolfter, and was fur-
‘ prifed that her women fhould fuffer a ftranger fo
‘ near her, when fhe faid to her, ‘ We think your ma-
‘ jefty very importunate to be fo ftubbborn in your
‘ defires of eating our fruits; but fince your life is in
‘ danger, my fifters and I have confented to give you
‘ as much as you can carry away, and to let you eat
‘ of them as long as you ftay here, provided you will
‘ make us one prefent.’ ‘ Ah! my good mother,
‘ (cried the queen) name it, I will give you my king-
‘ doms, heart, and foul, to have fome of the fruit: I
‘ cannot buy it too dear.’ ‘ We would have your
‘ majefty (faid fhe) give us the daughter you now
‘ bear in your womb. As foon as fhe is born, we will
‘ come and fetch her: fhe fhall be brought up by us,
‘ and we will endow her with all virtues, beauties, and
‘ fciences: in fhort, fhe fhall be our child, and we will
‘ make her happy: but your majefty muft obferve,
‘ that you muft never fee her any more till fhe is
‘ married. If you will agree to this propofition, I
‘ will cure you immediately, and carry you to our
‘ orchard, where, notwithftanding it is night, you
‘ fhall fee well enough to chufe what you would
‘ have; but if what I fay difpleafes your majefty,
‘ good-night.’ ‘ Though what you impofe on me,
‘ (replied the queen) is very hard, yet I accept it
‘ rather than die; for certainly, if I cannot live, my
‘ child muft be loft; therefore, fkilful fairy, (continued
‘ fhe) cure me, and let me not be a moment debarred
‘ of the privileges I am entitled to thereby.’

‘ The fairy touched her with a little golden wand,
‘ faying, ‘ Your majefty is free from all illnefs.’ And
‘ thereupon fhe feemed as if fhe had thrown off a heavy
‘ garment that had been very troublefome and incom-
‘ modious to her. She ordered all the ladies of her
‘ court to be called, and, with a gay air, told them fhe

was

‘ was extraordinary well, and would rise, since that the
‘ gates of the fairies palace, which were so strongly bar-
‘ rocaded, were set open for her to eat of the fruit, and
‘ carry what she pleased away. The ladies thought the
‘ queen delirious, and she was then dreaming of the
‘ fruit she longed so much for; insomuch, that instead
‘ of returning any answer, they fell a-crying, and
‘ called in the physicians; which delays put the queen
‘ into the utmost despair; she asked for her clothes, and
‘ they refusing her them, put her into a violent passion,
‘ which they looked upon as her fever. In the interim
, ‘ the physicians came, who, after having felt her pulse,
‘ and made their inquiries, could not deny but that she
‘ was in perfect health. The ladies seeing the fault they
‘ had committed through their great zeal, endeavoured
‘ to repair it by dressing her quickly. They every one
‘ begged her pardon, which she granted, and hastened
‘ to follow the old fairy, who waited for her. She went
‘ into the palace, where nothing was wanting to make
‘ it the finest in the world; which you will the more
‘ easily believe, sir, (added the new metamorphosed
‘ queen) when I shall tell you it was this we are now
‘ in. Two other fairies, not quite so old as she that
‘ conducted my mother, received her favourably at the
‘ gate; she desired them to carry her presently into the
‘ garden, and to those trees that bore the best fruits.
‘ They told her they were all equally good, and that
‘ unless she would have the pleasure of gathering them
‘ herself, they would call them too her. ‘ I beg, (said
‘ the queen) that I may have the satisfaction of seeing
‘ so extraordinary an event.’ Whereupon the elder of
‘ the three put her fingers in her mouth, and blowed
‘ three times; and then cried, apricots, peaches, necta-
‘ rines, plumbs, cherries, pears, melons, grapes, apples,
‘ oranges, lemons, gooseberries, currants, strawberries,
‘ rasberries, come all at my call.’ ‘ But, (said the
‘ queen) these fruits are not all ripe in the same season.’
‘ Oh, (said they) in our gardens we have all sorts of
‘ fruit always ripe and good, and they never diminish.’
‘ At

' At the fame time they came rolling to them with-
' out any bruifes; and the queen, who was impatient
' to fatisfy her longing, fell upon them, and took the
' firft that offered, which fhe rather devoured than eat.
' When her appetite was fomewhat fatisfied fhe defired
' the fairies to let her go to the trees, and have the
· ' pleafure to gather them herfelf: to which they gave
' their confent; but faid to her, at the fame time, you
' muft remember the promife you have made us; for
' you will not be allowed to run back from it. ' I
' am perfuaded, (replied fhe) that it is fo pleafant
' living with you, and this palace is fo charming, that
' if I did not love the king my hufband dearly, I would
' offer my felf; therefore you need not fear my retract-
' ing from my word. The fairies, who were very well
' fatisfied, opened the doors of their gardens and all
' their inclofures, and the queen ftayed in them three
' days and nights, without ever ftirring out, fo delici-
' ous fhe found them. She gathered fruit for her pro-
' vifion, and as they never wafted, loaded four hundred
' mules fhe brought along with her. The fairies added
' to their fruit, bafkets of gold of curious work, to carry
' them in, and many other very valuable rarities.
' They promifed to educate and make me a complete
' princefs, and to chufe me out an hufband, and to
' inform my mother of the wedding.

  ' The king was overjoyed at the queen's return,
' and all the court expreffed their pleafure to fee her
' again; there was nothing but balls, mafqueraces,
' and courfes, where the fruits the queen brought,
' ferved for delicious regales. The king prefered them
' before all other things, but knew not the bargain fhe
' had made with the fairies: but often afked her what
' country fhe had been in, to bring home fuch good
' things: to which fhe replied, fhe found them on a
' mountain that was almoft inacceffible; fometimes
' that fhe met with them in a valley, and fometimes in
' the midft of a garden or a great foreft: all which con-
' tradictions very much furprifed the king. He inquir-
' ed of thofe that went with her; but they were all for-
                                                ' bid

' bid to tell any thing of the matter. At length the
' queen, when her time was at hand, began to be trou-
' bled at what she had promifed the fairies, and grew
' very melancholy; she fighed every minute, and
' changed her countenance. The king was very much
' concerned, and preffed the queen to declare what was
' the caufe; who with fome difficulty told him what
' had paffed between her and the fairies, and that she
' had promife i them the daughter she was then big with.
' What! (cried the king) we have no children, and
' could you, who knew how much I defired them, for
' the eating of two or three apples, promife your
' daughter? certainly you muft have no regard for me.'
' and thereupon he loaded her with a thoufand re-
' proaches, which made my poor mother almoft ready
' to die for grief: but not content with this, he put her
' into a tower, under a ftrong guard, where she could
' have no converfation but with the officers that were
' appointed to attend her. The ill correfpondence be-
' tween the king and queen, put the court into the ut-
' moft confternation: they laid afide their rich clothes,
' and put on fuch as were agreeable to the general for-
' row. The king appeared for his part inexorable, and
' would not fee the queen; but as foon as I was born,
' made me be brought into the palace to be nurfed
' there, while my mother, at the fame time, remained a
' prifoner, and in an ill ftate of health. The fairies, who
' were not ignorant all this while of what was paffed,
' and who looked upon me as their own property, were
' fo provoked, that they refolved to have me; but be-
' fore they had recourfe to their art, they fent ambaf-
' fadors to the king, to defire him to fet the queen at
' liberty, and to reftore her to his favour again; and
' likewife to demand me, that I might be nurfed and
' brought up by them. The ambaffadors were fo little
' and deformed, for they were dwarfs, that the king,
' inftead of granting what they afked, refufed them
' rudely, and if they had not got away quickly, might
' have ferved them worfe.

                          ' When

' When the fairies were informed of my father's
' proceedings, they were so enraged, that after they
' had sent all the plagues capable of rendering his king-
' doms desolate, they let loose a terrible dragon that
' poisoned all the places wherever he came; devoured
' men, women and children, and killed all trees and
' plants with the breath of his nostrils. The king find-
' ing himself reduced to this extremity, consulted all
' the sages of his kingdom to know what he should do
' to preserve his subjects against these misfortunes
' wherewith they were oppressed: they advised him to
' send for the best physicians, to prescribe the most ex-
' cellent remedies, as one means: and to pardon all
' criminals that were condemned to die, if they would
' fight with the dragon, as the other. The king, who
' was well enough pleased with this advice, put it in
' execution, but received no benefit by it; for the mor-
' tality continued, and none fought with the dragon
' but were devoured: insomuch, that at last he had re-
' course to a fairy, who had protected him from his
' youth, and who was so old that she hardly ever rose
' from off her seat. He went to her, and reproached
' her for permitting his fate to persecute him in such a
' manner without giving him some assistance. ' What
' would you have me do, (replied the fairy) you have
' provoked my sisters, who have equal power with me,
' and we seldom act one against another; therefore
' think of appeasing them by giving your daughter,
' since they have a right to her; set the queen at liber-
' ty, who is too good and amiable to be used so ill, and
' resolve to fulfil what she had promised and then I'll
' assure you, you shall be happy.'

' The king my father loved me dearly: but seeing
' no other way to preserve his kingdoms, and to be de-
' livered from the fatal dragon, told his friend that he
' would believe her, and would give the fairies his daugh-
' ter, since she had assured him I should be taken care
' of, and treated as became a princess of my birth, and
' release the queen: and withal, desired her to tell him
' how he might send me to the fairy castle. ' You must
                                                 ' carry

' carry her (faid the fairy) in a cradle to the mountain
' of flowers, and muft ftay thereabouts to fee what hap-
' pens.'   The king told her fhe might acquaint her fif-
' ters that he and the queen would go with me thither
' in eight days time, and that they might do with me
' what they thought proper.

  ' As foon as he came back to the palace, he fent for
' the queen, with as much love and tendernefs as he had
' made her a prifoner with anger and paffion; but fhe
' was fo fa'len away and altered, that he could hardly
' know her, if he had not been very certain fhe was the
' perfon he once fo much doated on.   He begged of her,
' with tears in his eyes, to forget the ill treatment fhe
' had received from him, which he promifed her fhould
' be the laft.   She anfwered, that fhe had brought it on
' herfelf by her imprudence, in promifing her child to
' the fairies; and that if any thing would plead her
' excufe, it was the condition fhe was then in.   In fhort,
' he declared his defign to her of putting me into their
' hands; which fhe oppofed; and it feemed as if it
' was my fate to be always the caufe of my father and
' mother's difagreeing: But after fhe had cried and
' taken-on for fome time, without obtaining what fhe
' defired, (for my father too well forefaw the fatal con-
' fequences, and his fubjects ftill dying as if they had
' been guilty of our faults) fhe confented, and prepa-
' rations were made againft the ceremony.   I was put
' into a cradle of mother o'pearl, adorned as much as
' poffible by art, with garlands of flowers, feftoons hung
' round about it, and the flowers fo intermixed with
' jewels of feveral colours, that when the fun reflected
' upon them, they gave fuch a luftre that dazzled the
' eyes.   The magnificence of my drefs exceeded, if that
' was poffible, my cradle.   All the bands and rolls of
' my fwaddling cloaths were buckled with large pearls;
' four-and-twenty princeffes of the blood carried me
' on a kind of light litter, all dreffed in white, to refem-
' ble my innocence, and were followed by the whole
' court, according to their ranks.   While they were
' going up the mountain, they heard a melodious fym-
                            ' phony;

' phony? and afterwards fairies appeared to the num-
' ber of six-and-thirty, for the three had invited all
' their-friends, each in a shell of pearl, as large as that
' wherein Venus arose out of the sea, and drawn by
' sea horses, in as great pomp as if they had been the
' first queens in the world. They were exceeding old
' and ugly: They carried in their hands olive branches,
' to signify to the king, that by his submission he had
' gained their favour. When they took me, it was with
' such extraordinary caresses, that it seemed as if they
' lived only to make me happy.

' The dragon, which was the instrument of their
' revenge against my father, followed them bound in
' chains of diamonds. They took me in their arms,
' carressed me a thousand times, endowed me with
' several gifts, and then fell to dancing; and it is al-
' most incredible to believe how these old women
' jumped and skipped. Afterwards the devouring dra-
' gon came forwards, the three fairies, to whom my
' mother promised me, placed themselves upon him,
' and set my cradle between them; then striking the
' dragon with a wand, he presently displayed his large
' wings, which were as thin and fine as gauze, and in-
' termixed with various colours, and carried them to
' their castle. My mother seeing me in the air upon
' this furious dragon, could not forbear shrieking out,
' while the king comforted her by the assurance his
' friend had given him, that no ill accident should be-
' fall me, and that I should have as great care taken of
' me, as if I was in their own palace: Which assurance
' appeased her, though she was very much grieved to
' lose me for so long a time; especially when she re-
' flected that she herself was the cause of it. You must
' know, prince, (continued she) that my guardians
' built a tower on purpose for me, wherein there were
' a thousand beautiful apartments for all the seasons
' of the year, furnished with magnificent goods, and
' agreeable books; but there were no doors, and no
' other coming in but at the windows, which were pro-
' digious high. It was surrounded by beautiful gardens,
                                            ' full

' full of flowers, and embellished with fountains and
' arbours of greens, where it was cool and pleasant in
' the hottest seasons.   Here the fairies brought me up,
' and took more care of me than ever they promised
' the queen to do.   My cloaths were so fashionable
' and fine, that if any one had seen me, they would
' have thought it had been my wedding-day.   They
' taught me all that was proper for one of my age
' and birth to learn; and they had not much trouble
' with me, for there was nothing but what I com-
' prehended with great ease.   They were very well
' pleafed at my ready difpofition; and if I had never
' feen any body befides them, I fhould have been con-
' tented to have lived their all my life.   They came
' very often to fee me, mounted upon the fame dreadful
' dragon I have already fpoke of; they never men-
' tioned the king or queen to me, but called me their
' daughter, and I thought myfelf really fo.   No crea-
' ture lived with me in this tower, but a parrot and a
' little dog, which were endowed both with reafon and
' fpeech, and were given to divert me.

    '.One fide of the tower was built upon a hollow
' road, fet full of elms and other trees, which fhaded
' it fo much, that I never faw any one pafs by while
' I was there; when one day, as I was at the window,
' talking to my parrot and dog, I heard a noife, and
' looking about, perceived a young gentleman, who
' ftopped to hear our converfation.   I had never feen
' one before but in paintings, and was not forry that
' this accident had given me the opportunity; info-
' much, that not miftrufting the danger we run in the
' fatisfaction we received by the fight of fo lovely an
' object, I looked at him again, and the more I looked,
' the more pleafed I was.   He made me a low bow,
' fixed his eyes on me, and feemed concerned to know
' how to talk to me; for my windows being a great
' height, he was afraid of being heard, knowing that
' it was a caftle which belonged to fairies.   Night
' came upon us all on a fudden, or, to fpeak more
' properly, before we perceived; he founded his horn
                                                    twice

' twice or thrice, which he thought to please me with,
' and then went away without my discovering which
' way he took, it was so dark. I remained thoughtful:
' the pleasure I used to take in talking to my parrot
' and dog, was no ways agreeable. They said all the
' pretty things that could be to me, for these were
' very witty: but my thoughts were otherwise engaged,
' and I had not art enough to dissemble. My parrot
' observed all my actions; but made no mention of
' what he thought. The next morning I arose with the
' sun, and ran to my window, where I was most agree-
' ably surprised to see my spark, who was dressed mag-
' nificently: in which I flattered myself I had some
' share, and was not mistaken. He spoke to me
' through a speaking trumpet, told me he had been till
' that instant insensible to all the beauties he had be-
' held: but found himself so sensibly touched with me,
' that he could not live without seeing me. I was
' mightily pleased with his compliment, but vexed
' that I durst not make some reply; for I must have
' bawled out with all my might, and run the risque of
' being sooner heard by the fairies than him. I threw
' him some flowers I had in my hand, which he took
' for so signal a favour, that he kissed them several times,
' and thanked me. He asked me afterwards, if I ap-
' proved of his coming every day at the same hour
' under my window, and if I did, to throw something:
' whereupon I presently pulled off a torquoise ring,
' that I had on my finger, and cast it at him, making
' a sign for him to be gone presently, because I heard
' the fairy Violenta coming on the dragon to bring my
' breakfast.
    ' The first words she spoke, when she entered my
' chamber, were, ' I smell the voice of a man; a
' search, dragon.' Alas! what a condition was I in!
' I was ready to die with fear, lest he should find out,
' and follow my lover. Indeed, (said I) my good
' mamma, (for the fairy would be called so) you ban-
' ter, when you say you smell the voice of a man:
' can any one smell a voice? and should it be so, what
                                    ' wretch

' wretch could be fo bold as to venture coming up into
' this tower?   ' What you fay is very true, child,
' (faid fhe) I am overjoyed to hear you argue fo well:
' I fancy it is the hatred I have againſt men, that
' makes me think them nigh when they are not: how-
' ever, I have brought you your breakfaſt and a diſtaff;
' be fure fpin; yeſterday you did nothing, and my
' fiſters are very angry.'   (Upon my word I was fo
' taken up with this ſtranger, that I was not able to
' work.)   As foon as her back was turned, I threw away
' my diſtaff, and went upon the terrafs, to look as far
' as my eye would carry, in an excellent fpying-glaſs
' I had; by which, after having looked about fome
' time, I difcovered my lover under a rich pavillion
' of cloth of gold on the top of a high mountain, fur-
' rounded by a numerous court.   I doubted not but
' that he was fome neighbouring king's fon, and was
' afraid, left, when he came to the tower again, he
' ſhould be found out by the terrible dragon.   I went
' and fetched my parrot, and bid him fly to that moun-
' tain, to defire him, from me, not to come again,
' becaufe I was afraid my guardian ſhould difcover it,
' and he ſhould come into danger.   My parrot acquit-
' ted himfelf of his commiffion, and furprifed all the
' courtiers, to fee him come upon full wing, and perch
' upon the prince's ſhoulder, and whifper him foftly
' in the ear.   The prince was both overjoyed and
' troubled at this meffage; my care flattered his paffion .
' but the difficulty there was in fpeaking to me, gave
' him as much chagrin.   He afked the parrot a thou-
' fand queſtions, and the parrot him as many; for he
' was naturally inquifitive.   The prince in return
' for my torquoife, fent me a ring of another, but
' much finer than mine, cut in the ſhape of a heart,
' and fet round with diamonds; and told him (that
' he might treat him more like an ambaffador) he
' would prefent him with his picture, which he might
' ſhew to his charming miſtrefs.   The picture was tied
' under his wings, and the ring he brought in his bill.

' I waited

'I waited for the return of my green courtier, with
'an impatience unknown to me till then. He told
'me the person I sent him to was a great king, who
'had received him with all the joy possible; and
'that I might assure myself he lived only for me, and
'that though it was very dangerous for him to come
'so low as my tower, yet he was resolved to hazard
'all to see me. This news had such an effect upon
'me, that I fell a-crying. My parrot and dog com-
'forted me the best they could, for they loved me ten-
'derly: and then the parrot delivered the prince's ring
'to me, and shewed me his picture. I must own I was
'overjoyed that I could view so nigh a person I had
'never seen but at a distance. He appeared much
'more lovely than he seemed, and the different
'thoughts this sight inspired me with, for some were
'agreeable to me, and others not, made me very un-
'easy, which the fairies, when they come to see me,
'discovered. They said to one another, that I was cer-
'tainly troubled at something, and that they must
'think of providing a husband for me of the fairy race.
'They ramed several, but at last pitched on the little
'king Migonnet, whose kingdom lay about five hundred
'leagues off from their palace, but that was of no great
'importance. My parrot heard all their discourse,
'and came to give an account. ' Alas! my dear mis-
'tress, (said my bird) how much I pity you, if you
'should be king Migonnet's queen! he is enough to
'fright you, which I am sorry to tell you; but one
'thing I am sure of, the king who loves you, scorns to
'have such a one for his foot boy: and I think, (continu-
'ed he) if I am not much mistaken, I have perched upon
'the same bow with him.' How do you mean, (repli-
'ed I) on the same bow? ' Why, (said he) he has
'feet like an eagle.' I was very much afflicted at this
'account, I looked on the charming picture of the young
'king, and fancied he only gave it my parrot, that I
'might have an opportunity of seeing it, but when I
'compared it with Migonnet, I lost all hopes of life,
'and resolved to die sooner than marry him. I slept
'not all night, but talked with my parrot and dog, and
'towards

‘ towards morning began to clofe my eyes. My dog,
‘ who had a good nofe, fmelt the king at the foot of
‘ the tower: he awakened the parrot, and faid to him,
‘ I’ll engage the king is below.’ To which the parrot
‘ made anfwer, ‘ Hold thy tongue, thou prating fool;
‘ becaufe thy eyes and ears are always open, you are
‘ vexed that any body elfe fhould have reft.’ ‘ Well,
‘ faid the dog,) I am fure he is.   ‘ And, (replied the
‘ parrot) I am fure he is not: for I have, from my
‘ miftrefs, forbid him coming.’ ‘ You talk finely of
‘ your forbidding him ; (cried the dog) a man in love
‘ confults nothing but his paffions.’ Thereupon, pul-
‘ ling the parrot by the tale, he made fuch a noife that
‘ I awoke. They told me of their difpute, I ran or
‘ rather flew to the window, whence I faw the king hold-
‘ ing out his arms, who, by his trumpet, told me he
‘ could not live without me; that he poffeffed a
‘ flourifhing kingdom, and conjured me to find out
‘ fome way to efcape from my tower, or let him come
‘ to me; calling heaven and all the elements to witnefs,
‘ that he would marry me, and make me his queen.
‘ I bid my parrot go and tell him, that what he de-
‘ fired feemed almoft impoffible; that, however, upon
‘ the word he had given, and oaths he had fworn to me,
‘ I would endeavour to accomplifh his defires: but
‘ withal, to conjure him not to come every day, left he
‘ fhould be difcovered, which might prove fatal to us
‘ both.

‘ He went away, overjoyed with the flattering hopes
‘ I gave him. I found myfelf in the utmoft confufion,
‘ when I reflected on what I had promifed. I knew
‘ not how one fo young, timorous, and unexperienced,
‘ fhould get out of a tower, to which there were no
‘ doors, with the affiftance only of a dog and a parrot,
‘ therefore I refolved not to attempt a thing in which
‘ I could never fucceed, and fo fent my parrot to ac-
‘ quaint the king with it ; who was for killing himfelf that
‘ minute; but at laft charged the parrot to perfuade
‘ me to it, and to come and fee him die, or to bring
‘ him fome comfort. To which my winged ambaf-

F   fador

' fador anfwered, that he was very well perfuaded his
' miftrefs only wanted the power. When he gave me
' an account of what had happened, I was more grieved
' than ever. The fairy Violenta came, and found
' my eyes fwelled and red; fhe told me I had been
' crying, and if I did not tell her the reafon, fhe would
' burn me. I anfwered, trembling, I was weary with
' fpining, and that I had a great defire to make fome
' nets to catch fome birds, that deftroyed the
' fruit in the garden. ' What you defire, child
' (faid fhe) fhall coft you no more tears, I will bring
' you materials enough to-night; but I would rather
' you thought lefs of working, and more of fetting off
' your beauty, becaufe king Migonnet will be hear in
' a few days.' I fighed at this news, but made no re-
' ply; but as foon as her back was turned, began two
' or three rows of my nets, and afterwards applied my-
' felf to the making a ladder of ropes. But as the fairy
' had not furnifhed me with as much as I wanted,
' which obliged me to afk for more, fhe told me my
' work was like Penelope's web, it went not forwards,
' and yet I teafed her for more ftuff. O good mamma!
' (faid I) you may fay what you pleafe; but you muft
' know that as I am not very ready at this work, I burn
' it when it does not pleafe me. With which excufe
' fhe feemed fatisfied, and left me.
' I fent my parrot that night to bid the king come
' under my window, where he would find a ladder,
' and to tell him he fhould know more when he came;
' in fhort, I had tied it very faft, and was determined
' to efcape with him by this means; but he, as foon as
' he faw it, without waiting for my coming down,
' mounted up in hafte, and threw himfelf into my
' chamber, as I was making things ready for my flight.
' I was fo overjoyed to fee him, that I forgot the danger
' we were in. He renewed all his oaths, and entreated
' me to defer his happinefs no longer: we made my
' parrot and dog the witneffes of our marriage, which
' was the moft private in the world for perfons of our
' rank, and none certainly were ever better fatisfied.
The

' The king left me before day: I told him of the fairies
' defign to marry me to Migonnet, and gave him a
' defcription of his mean and forry figure, for which his
' horror was as great as mine. As foon as the king
' was gone, the hours feemed like years; I ran to the
' window, and followed him with my eyes, notwith-
' ftanding the darknefs; but how great was my furprife
' to fee a fiery chariot drawn in the air, by fix winged
' falamanders, who flew fo fwift, that the eye was not
' able to follow them. This chariot was attended
' by a great many guards, all mounted on oftriches.
' I did not give myfelf time to think that it was Mi-
' gonnet that was thus traverfing the air, but I believed
' it was a fairy, or inchanter. Soon after, the fairy
' Violenta came into my chamber, and told me fhe
' brought me good news, that my lover would be with
' me prefently, and bid me prepare myfelf to receive
' him: and with that gave me fine clothes and jewels
' But pray, (faid I) who has informed you that I want
' to be married? I am fure it is the fartheft from my
' thoughts; therefore fend king Migonnet back again:
' for I will not put in one pin more, whether he thinks
' me handfome or not? I am not for him. ' Oh! oh!
' (faid the fairy again) little rebel, little empty-pate,
' I fhall not mind your raillery, but I fhall ———'
' What will you do? (replied I, enraged at the names
' fhe had called me) can any one be worfe ferved than
' I am, to live all my days immured with a parrot and
' a dog, and to be vifited conftantly by that frightful
' dragon? ' Ha! ingrate! (faid the fairy) is this all
' we deferve for our care and pains; I have told my
' fifters but too often, we fhould have but forry recom-
' penfe.' At this fhe went away, and told them of our
' difference, which put them into no little amazement.
   ' My parrot and dog remonftrated to me, that if I
' fhould continue any longer thus fturdy, they forefaw
' that I fhould undergo fome misfortune. But I was
' fo proud of poffeffing the heart of a king, that I def-
' pifed both the fairies, and the advice of thofe my
' little companions. I would not drefs me; but ftrove
               F 2   ' all

‘ all I could to tumble my head-drefs, that I might ap-
‘ pear lefs agreeable to Migonnet. We had an inter-
‘ view upon the terrafs, he came in his fiery chariot ;
‘ but of all dwarfs, he was the leaft I ever faw in my
‘ life. His feet were like an eagle’s, and clofe to his
‘ knees, for legs he had none. His royal garment was
‘ not above half a yard long, and trailed one third part
‘ upon the ground. His head was as big as a peck, and
‘ his nofe long enough for twelve birds to perch on it,
‘ and be regailed at the fame time with a delightful bufh,
‘ for his beard was large enough for canary birds to
‘ build their nefts in: and for his ears, they reached
‘ a foot above his head, but were a great part hid by a
‘ high crown that he wore to appear more grand. The
‘ flame of his chariot coddled the fruit, withered the
‘ flowers, and dried up the fountains of the gardens.
‘ He came with open arms to embrace me, and I ftood
‘ upright, which obliged his firft ’fquire to hold him up.
‘ As foon as he came near to me, I ran to my chamber,
‘ and faftened my window: fo that Migonnet enraged,
‘ was forced to retire to the fairies, who afked a thou-
‘ fand pardons for the affront ; and to appeafe him be-
‘ caufe he was powerful, they refolved to bring him at
‘ night into my chamber, and while I was afleep, to
‘ tie my hands and feet, and put me into his chariot.
‘ Things being thus agreed on, they only chided me for
‘ what I had done, and charged me to think of making
‘ him amends for the future. Which mildnefs of theirs
‘ furprifed my parrot and dog, who told me their hearts
‘ mifgave them, for they knew the fairies to be ftrange
‘ ill-tempered fort of old ladies, and efpecially Violenta.
‘ I laughed at their fears, and waited with the utmoft
‘ impatience for my dear hufband, whofe defires to fee
‘ me again were no lefs violent: I threw out the ladder
‘ of ropes, refolving to efcape with him, he came foftly
‘ up it, and faid a thoufand kind things, which I dare
‘ not recall to my remembrance.
  ‘ While we were talking to gether, with the fame tran-
‘ quillity as if it had been in his own palace, he faw all
‘ on a fudden the windows broke open, and the fairies
                                            ‘ enter

' enter upon their frightful dragon, followed by Migon-
' net in his fiery chariot, and all his guards on oftriches.
' The king, without any difmay, clapped his hand on
' his fword, and thought of fecuring and protecting me;
' when thefe barbarous creatures fet their dragon upon
' him, which devoured him before my face. Vexed,
' and in defpair, I threw myfelf into the mouth of this
' dreadful monfter, that he might fwallow me as he had.
' done the prince, who was dearer to me than all the
' world befides. And I had certainly undergone the fame
' fate; but the fairies, who were more cruel than the
' monfter, would not permit it, but faid, I muft be
' referved for greater punifhments; a quick death was
' too mild a one for fo bafe a creature: whereupon
' touching me, I found myfelf changed into a White Cat.
' They conducted me to this ftately palace, which be-
' longed to my father, and turned all the lords and
' ladies into cats; and for the reft of his jubjects, left
' of them only the hands, which we fee, and reduced
' me to that miferable condition you found me: let-
' ting me know at the fame time my birth, the death of
' my father and mother, and that I never fhould be re-
' leafed from this metamorphofis, but by a prince that
' perfectly refembled my hufband, who they deprived me
' of. You fir, have that refemblance, the fame features,
' air and voice: I was ftruck as foon as I faw you, and
' was informed of all that fhould happen, and am ftill
' of all that fhall come to pafs: my pains will be at an
' end.' ' And fhall mine, fair queen, (faid the prince)
' be of long duration?' ' I love you, fir, already more
' than my life, (faid the queen) we muft go to your
' father and know his fentiments for me, and whether
' he will confent to what you defire.' After this fhe
went out, the prince handed her into a chariot, which
was much more magnificent than that fhe had, and
then went into it himfelf. All the reft of the equipage
anfwered it fo well, that the buckles of the horfes har-
neffes were diamonds and emeralds. I fhall fay no.
thing of their converfation, which muft be very polite,

fince

since she was not only a great beauty, but also a great wit; and for the prince, he was no ways inferior to her therein: so that all their thoughts were bright and lively.

When they came nigh the castle where the brothers were to meet, the queen went into a cage of crystal set in gold, which had curtains drawn about it, that she might not be seen, and was carried by handsome young men richly clothed. The prince staid in the chariot, and saw his brothers walking with two princesses of extraordinary beauty. As soon as they knew him, they came to receive him, and asked him if he had brought a mistress along with him; to which he answered, that he had been so unfortunate in all his journey, to meet with none, but what were very ugly; but that he had brought a pretty White Cat. 'A cat, (said they, 'laughing) what was you afraid that mice should de- 'vour our palace?' The prince replied, that he was not very wise in making such a present to his father, but it was the greatest rarity he could meet with. Afterwards they all bent their course towards the capital town. The two elder princes and the princesses went in calashes of blue embossed with gold, with plumes of white feathers upon the horses heads; nothing was finer than this cavalcade. The younger prince followed after, and then the cage of crystal, which every body admired. The courtiers crowded to tell the king that the princes were arrived, and brought most beautiful ladies along with them; which news was no ways pleasing to the king. The two eldest princes were very earnest to shew him the beauties they had brought, whom he received kindly, but knew not in whose favour to decide; when looking on the youngest, 'What (said he) are you 'come by yourself?' 'Your majesty, (replied the 'prince) will find in this cage a pretty little cat, which 'mews and plays so sweetly, that you will be very well 'pleased with her.' Hereat, the king smiled, and was going to open the cage; but as soon as he approached towards it, the queen with a spring broke it in pieces, and appeared like the sun when it breaks fourth

from

from a cloud. Her fine hair was fpread upon her fhoulders, and laid in fine large rings, and her forehead was adorned with flowers. Her gown was a thin white gaufe, lined with a rofe coloured taffety. She made the king a low courtefy, who in the excefs of his admiration could not forbear crying out, ' This is the in-' comparable fairy who deferves my crown.' ' Sir, ' (faid fhe) I came not to rob you of your crown, which ' you wear fo worthily: I was born heirefs to fix king-' doms, give me leave to prefent one of them to you, ' and one to either of your fons, for which I afk no other ' return but your friendfhip, and this young prince in-' marriage: thiee kingdoms will be enough for us.' The king and all the court were not able to exprefs ' their joy and amazement. The marriages of the three princes and their princeffes were celebrated at the fame time, and the court fpent feveral months in pleafures and diverfions; after which they all went to their dominions, and the White Cat gained as great honour by her bounty and generofity, as by her rare merrit and beauty.

F I N I S.